It was wonderful to have a famous master.

"Very good, Kiyoi," said Sensei. "You used something sharp in the brush just now, like the edge of a knife. The brush is many things. Remember that edge."

He was right. There was something sharp in the brush, and I could cut a straight or curved line with a quick turn of my wrist. And the amount of ink on the brush had a lot to do with what you could do with it. I felt as if I was learning calligraphy all over again....

At noon Sensei sent me to a restaurant to order our lunch.

"Noro Shinpei's place?" asked the woman who looked like the owner's wife.

"Yes, we'd like three bowls of noodles with shrimp, please."

"We haven't seen you before, have we?"

"No, I'm new."

"What happened to Tokida-san?"

"He's working with Sensei. I'm the new pupil."

"What, another one?" The woman looked me up and down. "But you seem so young. You must be awfully good to be his student."

Even the owner came out of the kitchen to inspect me. It was wonderful to have a famous master.

"For those of us who have marveled at Allen Say's talent through the years, we thank Sensei who helped send Kiyoi on this marvelous journey to us."

—*The Children's Book Review*

OTHER PUFFIN BOOKS YOU MAY ENJOY

THE
INK-KEEPER'S
APPRENTICE

❖ ❖ ❖ ❖ ❖

Allen Say

PUFFIN BOOKS

I am grateful to Nina Ignatowicz
for having persuaded me to write this book.
—A.S.

PUFFIN BOOKS
Published by the Penguin Group
Penguin Books USA Inc., 375 Hudson Street, New York, New York 10014, U.S.A.
Penguin Books Ltd, 27 Wrights Lane, London W8 5TZ, England
Penguin Books Australia Ltd, Ringwood, Victoria, Australia
Penguin Books Canada Ltd, 10 Alcorn Avenue, Toronto, Ontario, Canada M4V 3B2
Penguin Books (N.Z.) Ltd, 182-190 Wairau Road, Auckland 10, New Zealand

Penguin Books Ltd, Registered Offices: Harmondsworth, Middlesex, England

First published in the United States of America by Harper & Row, 1979
Second edition published in the United States
of America by Houghton Mifflin Company, 1994
Published in Puffin Books, 1996

3 5 7 9 10 8 6 4 2

Text copyright © Allen Say, 1979
Introduction copyright © Allen Say, 1994
All rights reserved

Puffin Books ISBN 0-14-037826-X

Printed in the United States of America

To my daughter, Yuriko

FOREWORD

❖ ❖ ❖ ❖ ❖

This book was first published in 1979. Since then I have illustrated nine picture books, writing six of them myself. Looking back on this small body of work, I see that my stories are essentially autobiographic. I did not plan this consciously, but *The Ink-keeper's Apprentice* set the tone. So in this reissue of my homage to my great teacher (sensei), Noro Shinpei, I decided to give my real name to the narrator. In Japanese it has three syllables, Seii, but the last i is usually dropped. My father had adopted the English spelling long ago, and over the years I've become attached to this hybrid of a name.

In 1982, I returned to Japan for my first-grade class reunion and discovered that my mentor, with whom I had lost contact for twenty-five years, was alive and well. We met in a Tokyo cafe and talked of the old days. His wife had died a few years before, and his grown children had left home. Tokida, my fellow apprentice, had returned to Osaka and was not heard from again. I reminded Sensei of the lesson he had taught me, that to draw is to discover. "And to be astonished," he now added. Then he led me to a well-known Shinto shrine and bade me to make a wish. When I left him, he said he had prayed that I would become a great artist. I had prayed that Sensei would live a long life.

Last year, when *Grandfather's Journey* was published, I sent him the first copy I received from my publisher. And Sensei replied:

> *Thank you for the book. When I opened the package and saw the cover, I swallowed a breath. It is a splendid work. The boy who used to run around on the roof of the inn where I worked has become a mature artist. Next year I will be an old man of eighty, but I plan to go on living awhile, to watch your craft deepen.*

Allen Say, 1994

ONE

✦ ✦ ✦ ✦ ✦

ENGLISH CONVERSATION SCHOOL, said a small hand-painted sign on the door. I looked at the crumpled newspaper article in my hand to check the address, and my heart sank. No mistake, I'd come to the right place.

I had never been in this part of Tokyo, and the shabbiness of the neighborhood depressed me. The dead-end street was full of cracks and puddles, and the two-storied office building in front of me looked more like a run-down barracks than a place of business. I looked blankly at the rain-soaked side shingles and thought of rows and rows of decaying teeth stacked on top of one another. The place just didn't seem like the home of the great man I'd come to meet.

Suddenly a deafening noise exploded, and the screeching sound of electricity drowned me. The large speaker of a nearby movie theater began to blast away the theme music, announcing the start of the first afternoon show. I looked back toward the bustling train station where I'd gotten off a train only a few minutes before, and wondered if I should go back. Bicycles darted every which way, enormous shiny American cars cruised like the lords of the avenue, charwomen rummaged among the ruins of bombed buildings to bag whatever trash they could find. In between the blasts from the speaker I heard the calls of the shoe-shine boys, and felt a chill. I didn't know what to do.

I stood there a good five minutes, hoping for someone to come out of the building — for anything to happen. But nobody came out, and nothing happened. Finally, more to get away from the noise than anything else, I rushed through the front door.

The long hallway was dark and empty, smelling of mildew. The evenly spaced doors along the corridor had windows of milky glass, and ghostlike figures moved behind them, whispering in small, dull voices. I went from door to door, reading the nameplates, but the man I was looking for was not on the first floor. It was almost a relief.

The second floor wasn't much better, except a dirty skylight in the ceiling cast a shaft of light along the corridor and made the place seem a little more cheerful. Another ENGLISH CONVERSA-TION SCHOOL sign was posted on the wall at the top of the stair-case, with an arrow pointing to the far end of the hallway. I followed the arrow, and went past the school until there was only one door left. Something small and white glowed on the door, right below the frosted glass. It was an ordinary calling card, pinned there with a thumbtack.

Noro Shinpei, read the four characters. At first glance the name looked like any other, but when it was read aloud it was nonsense. Noro, the surname, means slow, and Shinpei is an army private. Slow Army Private. It was obviously a pen name, but it looked very official and dignified on a printed card. I looked at it again and touched the crisp card to see if it was real. My heart began to beat fast, then I laughed silently. Not because of the comical name, but because I'd finally found the man I'd come to meet.

Feeling weak in my knees, I tapped twice on the glass.

"Enter," said a man's voice. It was more like an order than an invitation. I cracked open the door and peeked inside. Two figures were seated at a long desk, peering up at me with curiosity.

"A-are you Master Noro?"

"You've found him. Come in and close the door before you catch TB."

Quickly I closed the door and looked around the room. Books and magazines and pieces of paper were scattered everywhere. The desk was cluttered with tins of cigarettes, glass ashtrays brimming with butts, pens and nibs and pencils, brushes of all sizes, and more inkpots than anybody could use in a lifetime.

"The squalor impresses you." Noro Shinpei smiled. His two front teeth were crowned with gold.

"No, sir. I mean it looks fine, sir," I said with a shaky voice.

"We had a visit from the local authorities this morning. The police, you know," he said and laughed. "Well, pull up a chair and sit. Put the books on the floor, anywhere. Hand me a cigarette, Tokida," he told the youth sitting next to him. I put the pile of books on the floor and sat down.

Noro Shinpei was in his late thirties. His long hair looked as if it was always combed with fingers, and he wore a long, cotton-filled winter kimono. Not many men wore kimonos anymore and he looked old-fashioned, sitting there with his hands inside the long sleeves, samurai-style. There was something about Noro Shinpei that reminded me of an old-time *ronin*. I say old-time because in the old days a *ronin* was a samurai without a master. A samurai was a warrior, an expert swordsman who dedicated his life to serving a master. Today a *ronin* is someone without a job.

Tokida looked three or four years older than me. His hair was cropped close to the skull, and his sharp face was full of pimples. He wore a pair of round steel-rimmed glasses, and his shirt was crinkled as if he'd slept in it. He stared at me suspiciously and lit a cigarette. I was impressed.

"And your name?" asked Noro Shinpei.

"Sei, sir."

"That's an unusual name. How do you write that?"

3

I wrote the two characters on a piece of paper.

"Kiyoi." He misread my name.

"It's Sei, sir." I corrected him.

"And what can I do for you?"

"I want to be a cartoonist, sir."

"I see. . . ."

A long pause.

"And you want to be my pupil, is that it?"

"Yes, sir."

Tokida blew a big smoke ring out of his puckered mouth. My ears felt hot and the shirt collar tightened around my neck.

"How old are you, Kiyoi?"

"Thirteen, sir. I'll be fourteen in August."

"How tall are you?" He looked me up and down in disbelief.

"A hundred and seventy-three meters, sir."

"Centimeters, you mean."

"Yes, sir."

"Remarkable. A giraffe-boy, the chosen one," he said. He was being polite, punning on giraffe-child which also means a wonder child. Telephone pole was what they called me at school.

"Where do you go to school?"

"Aoyama Middle School, sir."

"A very good school. Is this spring vacation?"

"Yes, sir, two weeks."

"Where do you live?"

"Shibuya, sir."

"Near your school. Were you born in Tokyo, then?"

"Yokohama, sir."

"Do your parents know you came to see me?"

"Yes, sir."

"Did you tell them why?"

"Yes, they don't mind, sir."

"You're quite sure about that? Even if you are a genius, you're a minor and I have to respect your parents' wishes. What is your father's occupation?"

"He's a merchant, sir."

4

"Now that's a sly answer. He could be anything from a street peddler to a department store tycoon. I get the feeling you're the oldest son."

"Yes, sir."

"Where is your sense of filial duty?"

"What do you mean, sir?"

"What does your father feel about his heir wanting to become a cartoonist?"

"He doesn't mind, sir, he really doesn't. He only wants me to stay in school. He says I'm going to change my mind when I grow older," I said desperately.

"And do you think you'll change your mind?"

"No, sir," I admitted.

"Of course not. At least that's what you think now. What about your mother?"

"She doesn't mind either, sir, as long as I do well in school."

"You're blessed with a wise mother. Do you know what a good policeman is?"

"No, sir."

"He's a man who thinks everyone is a criminal. Consider your neighbor to be a thief. Do you know that saying?"

"Yes, sir."

"Do you know what a bad policeman is?"

"No, sir."

"A man who regards all artists as criminals," he said, drawing long on a fresh cigarette. "So tell me, why do you want to be a cartoonist?"

The question surprised me. Somehow I didn't expect such a question from a famous cartoonist.

"I'm not sure, sir, but I've always drawn. I'm not good at anything else. I'd rather draw cartoons than anything, sir."

"Drawing before dumplings." He rephrased an old saying. "Tell me, if your father were to forbid you to take up cartooning, what would you do?"

"I would do it anyway, sir."

"And if I don't take you on, what will you do?"

5

"I don't know. . . . I'll do it on my own, sir," I said defiantly, though I suddenly felt tired and hopeless.

"I like your spirit," he said and began to laugh. His laughter took me aback.

"So what have you been drawing?"

"I've been copying mostly, sir. I've copied a lot from your strips."

"Draw something for me then," he said, handing me a drawing pad. "Let's say a horse. Yes, draw a horse, and don't try to imitate my style — or anybody else's for that matter. I want you to draw it in your own way. Tokida and I will go about our business, so relax and take your time."

I didn't move. I couldn't. My knees would have buckled under me if I tried to stand up. I picked up a pencil and licked the lead. I wished Tokida would leave the room, but he showed no sign of getting up. He's probably enjoying the scene, I thought, waiting for me to make a fool of myself. What if my hand shakes, I thought suddenly. Then I heard the theater speaker for the first time since I'd been in the room. The noise was faint, but the mumbling dialogue and the background music comforted me.

The first thing I drew was an ear, the side view of it, then I drew another ear, slightly overlapping the first. Then the slanting line of the forehead, a little bump over the eye, and the dipping "dish nose" of an Arabian horse. I heard the soft lead of the pencil sliding over the paper. My hand didn't shake, and I wasn't afraid anymore.

Soon a side view of a horse appeared on the page. I could have drawn the horse from some other angle but didn't think of it. I was happy with the way the horse was coming out. The snout was about the right length, the legs had all the joints, the tail turned out a little too bushy, and the eye was a bit like a human eye, but it was a horse, all right, and not a bad one. I shaded the animal here and there and handed the drawing to the great cartoonist.

He looked at it through thick coiling cigarette smoke, squinting his eyes. He had a very large nose for a Japanese, pitted with pores,

6

and his jowl was blue though it was freshly shaven. Maybe he's part Ainu, I thought, one of those people who lived in Japan long before the Chinese and the Koreans came to claim the land for themselves.

Tokida craned his neck to peek at my drawing but the cartoonist closed the sketchbook.

"The horse was an excuse," he said. "I wanted to see how you draw. Most boys your age draw like this," he said, drawing a straight line with many jerky strokes. "You seem to have survived your art teachers."

I thought he was paying me a compliment, but wasn't sure, so I said nothing.

"So you want to devote your life to the serious business of cartooning," he asked.

"Yes, sir."

"What can I do to dissuade you?"

"Nothing, sir."

"Then I have no choice but to take you on."

"You mean I can be your pupil, sir?"

"If that is what you want."

Speechless, I nodded my head like an imbecile.

"Then I accept you as my pupil. But there's one thing, Kiyoi. Any talk about money and out you go; is that clear?"

"Yes, sir."

"Don't worry, Kiyoi, I'll make you earn your keep." He laughed. "Tokida here is three years older than you. At least that's what he tells me. Think of him as your partner, an older brother."

Tokida gave me a thin smile. I knew very well he resented me for barging in to share his master. I had read about him in the paper, the youngest budding cartoonist.

"If you have nothing else to do, stay for supper," said my new master.

"Thank you, sir, but my family is expecting me," I lied, and bowed several times to the two of them and walked out of the door as calmly as I could. I floated down the dusty staircase, swam through the hallway, and burst out the front door.

Puddles were still there on the pavement, but now the rainbow of the oil slick caught my eye. The speaker was still blasting away, but now it sounded as though it was celebrating my triumph. I looked up at the ugly building and somehow the shabbiness of it seemed wonderful.

TWO

Grandmother was surprised to see me. I didn't visit her often, except to receive my monthly allowance and to see my mother when she visited her once a month. Grandmother was wearing her usual dark kimono. Even in the heat of summer she would always wear dark garments. She was a tiny woman, but in spite of her fragile appearance her steely eyes frightened many people.

"Why do you waste your money on such things?" she said when I handed her the box of chestnut cakes.

"I thought you might enjoy them, Grandmother," I said, knowing her weakness for them. Not even her usual gruffness was going to annoy me today.

"Shall I make a pot of tea for you?" I asked.

"Put the kettle on; I will pour the tea," she said.

Grandmother never allowed anybody to pour tea in her house. Besides, I was not good at it. I went into the kitchen and saw two gleaming sardines on a piece of newspaper by the sink. A bunch of spinach lay next to the fish.

"Stay for supper," she ordered when I joined her in the tea room.

"I can't, Grandmother, I'm only staying for a few minutes."

"One would think you had something important to do. And what's the occasion? Why the visit?" she asked suspiciously.

"No occasion. I thought I'd come and see how you are. I'm in good health, and I still have most of the money you gave me."

"Don't be fresh. You're too thin. Not eating properly. And look how pale you are."

"I've been studying too hard," I said.

"Ha! That's what you say. Drawing again, I'm sure. I didn't give you permission to live alone so that you could draw silly pictures. Studying too hard, indeed. I wept over your last report card, Koichi. I wanted to crawl into a hole, when I looked at your dreadful scores in front of all the other parents. Dreadful!"

"I'm trying my best, Grandmother, really I am. Have you heard from Mother?" I changed the subject.

"Yes. She'll be here at the end of the month. She's a hardworking woman, Koichi."

"Yes, I know," I said, and opened the package of sweets. Grandmother could never resist the jellied chestnuts. I got the kettle of boiling water from the kitchen and Grandmother took out the tea things from the cupboard. She poured the hot water into one pot, let it cool for a moment, and then poured it into another pot with tea leaves in it. It was always the same. Grandmother sipped the brew noisily. Drinking tea was one of the few things that made her happy. She bit into a chestnut cake and for a moment I thought her eyes softened. I felt like I was watching a tiger. She would never be more relaxed than now. I took a chance.

"Grandmother, have you ever heard of Noro Shinpei?" I asked her.

"What kind of name is that?"

"A pen name. He's a famous cartoonist."

"What a disrespectful name. Slow Soldier . . . it's not even amusing. Slow Soldier? Was there something about him in the paper recently? And a boy from Osaka?"

"Yes, the same one," I said quickly. "Tokida is the boy's name. Do you remember, he walked for sixteen days to come to Tokyo and Sensei — I mean, Noro Shinpei." In my mind I was already beginning to refer to Noro Shinpei as a sensei, a master.

"Yes, I remember," said Grandmother. "It was an unusual story. Why do you ask?"

"No reason. I wondered if you know who he is. I think he's the best cartoonist there is."

"And who cares about a cartoonist?"

"Don't you think I should become a cartoonist?" I asked.

"Don't talk rubbish. Your mother is not sending you to a good school so you can draw silly pictures. A cartoonist, indeed! Remember your blood, Koichi."

"I'm only joking," I said.

That was her favorite expression, Remember your blood. She came from an old samurai family. So had Grandfather. His ancestors had been proud warriors for four hundred years. But the Second World War had made my grandparents paupers. Grandfather was dead now. My mother was supporting Grandmother and me. And Grandmother still held on to old traditions. Such things as a good family name, genteel upbringing, and good schooling were important to her. And most of all, our lineage.

Suddenly I wanted to leave Grandmother's house at once. I *had* to tell someone about my sensei.

"May I take another set of sheets?" I asked. "I think there's an extra set upstairs." Grandmother nodded without looking up.

I went upstairs to the small six-mat room and found a set of sheets and a pillowcase in the closet. The room was the way I'd left it almost a year ago. It had been my room since I'd come to Tokyo to go to school, and now the only trace of my stay there was some thumbtack holes in the wall where I used to pin my drawings.

"Stay for supper; I bought two fish today," said Grandmother when I came downstairs.

"Thank you, but I really should be going," I said, and looked at my watch. "I have some studying to do."

"I thought this was spring vacation."

"Yes, but they gave us a lot of homework."

"Do as you wish. But make sure you eat something."

"Yes, I will. I'll see you at the end of the month," I said, and left her.

It was a great relief to leave Grandmother's house. Sometimes I felt like shouting at her. I didn't know why I had gone to see her in the first place. I was used to being alone, but today I felt the need to talk to someone. Grandmother was the only relative I had in Tokyo, and I didn't have a close friend. I had thought perhaps there was a chance Grandmother would understand that I wanted to be a cartoonist. I should have known better.

But even so, nothing could dampen my spirits. Perhaps Grandmother will soften someday, I thought as I walked on the busy street toward the train station. I traced in my mind every detail of Sensei's studio, repeated some of the things he had said, and chuckled to myself.

For no reason I stopped in front of a restaurant and stared absentmindedly at the sample dishes in the window. There were rows of plastic noodles, meats, and fish cakes made out of rubbery material, looking ghastly in the milky light of fluorescent lamps. Ordinarily the sight would have sickened me, but suddenly I felt hungry. I'll order the most expensive dish, I said to myself, and walked in.

❖ ❖ ❖

It was dark when I got home. I squeezed around my bicycle that took up most of the porch, kicked off my shoes, and went in. I'd been living there by myself since I'd left Grandmother's house. The square eight-mat room, about twelve by twelve feet, had a flush toilet by the porch, a washbasin, a tiny closet, and a big sliding window. There were no cooking facilities so I ate all my meals out. It was housing for the poor, the kind of place the old-time residents of Tokyo used to call the eel's bed.

With a good deal of satisfaction I looked around my room in the harsh light of the naked bulb hanging from the ceiling. It was quiet. The only noise came from the round alarm clock with two bells on top, beating like my heart. I looked in the chipped mirror above the washbasin and grinned at myself. Then I filled the kettle and turned the hot plate on. Grandmother had given them to me; she said the hot plate would keep me warm on cold winter nights.

I lit a candle and turned out the overhead light, and thought about the day. Often I read the books I liked by candlelight. Grandmother would never have allowed it. Also she never let me stay up late. It was good to live alone.

I had nearly fallen asleep at my desk when I heard a knock on my door. It was my next-door neighbor, Mr. Kubota. There was a slight tinge of red around his eyes. Drinking, I thought. He was about twenty-one, and his short hair was always neatly parted in the center. He was studying literature at a university, and he also held a second-degree black belt in karate. I had been to his room several times and had beer with him, but this was the first time he came to see me.

"How goes it, Sei-san?" he asked. "Something the matter with your lights?"

"No, I was just thinking," I said, turning on the overhead light. "Can I pour a cup of tea for you?"

"No, thank you, that would sober me up. I'm on my way to the Ginza. A little drinking with some bad friends, you know. I saw your candle burning and thought you'd blown a fuse or something."

Suddenly I thought of Sensei.

"Mr. Kubota, you know who Noro Shinpei is, don't you?"

"The cartoonist?"

"Yes. I'm his pupil."

"What do you mean?"

"I went to see him today and asked him if I could study with him and he said yes."

"Remarkable. Wait a minute, I'll be right back," he said and was gone. In a moment he was back with a half-filled bottle of port wine.

"This calls for a celebration. Here, have some, it'll get your

13

circulation going." He handed me the bottle. I poured him some wine in a teacup.

"Tell me what happened," he said as he drank from the large cup. I told him about Sensei with great excitement. It was wonderful to have a good listener.

"Remarkable," he said again. "I feel as though I'm hearing a story from another age — master and disciple. If you want to learn something, seek out a master. Congratulations. Enjoy what's left in the bottle; I must be off," he said and left me.

I returned to my desk and looked in my diary for the entry I'd made the night I'd moved into the apartment.

I am going to be a famous cartoonist, read the entry.

THREE

The next day I arrived at the studio at ten in the morning. Sensei and Tokida were already at work, sitting in the same places, wearing the same clothes. Sensei's small eyes were bloodshot and his face bristled with a heavy beard.

"You've come just in time to give us a hand. Tokida and I have been going nonstop since you left. Have you had breakfast?"

"Yes, sir."

"Pour yourself a cup of tea. A magazine reporter is coming over at two to pick up this installment. We'll relax after that. Here, I'll have another cup," he said and handed me his mug. Already I was beginning to feel useful, pouring tea for the master.

"Ready to work, Kiyoi?" Tokida spoke to me for the first time.

"Yes, what can I do?"

"Don't worry, you'll have plenty to do. You don't know what you got yourself into," Tokida said. He spoke with a slight Osaka accent, which is softer and more melodious than the sharp, staccato speech of the Tokyo natives.

It was exciting, and a little eerie, to watch one of the best-known comic serials come to life in front of me. Tokida penciled in the frames on thick bristol boards with a ruler, and Sensei sketched in the rough figures with a soft-leaded pencil. He drew with tremendous speed and energy. Even when his pencil wasn't touching the paper his hand moved round and round as if drawing hundreds of small circles. I kept looking at his hand and noticed a pea-sized callus on the middle finger, and I wondered how many hundreds of hours I had to draw to work up a callus like Sensei's. I looked at Tokida's drawing hand and saw a budding pea, stained yellow from tobacco. Then I saw that half of the little finger on Tokida's left hand had been lopped off.

Sensei didn't draw in any orderly way, but skipped from one frame to the next, as if he was working on his favorite scenes first. A steady stream of ideas seemed to rush through his head and flow out from the tip of his pencil. How did he know what size to make the balloons before putting in the words? I wondered, but was afraid to ask.

Sometimes the bristol boards became so heavily penciled it was hard to tell what was going on. Sensei would scribble a few words here and there inside the balloons and chuckle to himself. Then he would put a new nib in a pen holder and start to ink over the drawings. He used the pen as quickly and freely as he did a pencil, except with the pen he never went over the same line twice. He worked so fast I was afraid he might ruin a drawing, but he never did. The nib slid over the smooth paper effortlessly, and the gleaming streak of black ink flowed with ease and power. Suddenly a cartoon figure would emerge, almost leaping out of the page. It took my breath away.

"Do you know what a baseball player's uniform looks like?" asked Sensei.

Tokida and I looked at each other and nodded.

"Draw one for me."

It's another test, I thought. Tokida seemed as puzzled as I was, but we each drew a baseball uniform. Sensei glanced at our drawings.

"So you thought you knew what it looks like," he said. "You hardly know anything about it. You don't know where the seams come together, you're not sure about the length of the sleeves, and you don't know how many loops there are to hold up the pants. Soon I'm going to have you draw the backgrounds, and I want you to know what it is that you're drawing. For instance, when I ask you to draw a Shinto temple, I don't mean just any old temple, but a Shinto temple. Most of the time no one will know the difference, but I want *you* to know it. If you're not sure, look it up; don't rely on your memory."

Tokida and I said nothing. When Sensei asked us to draw the uniform I thought he was being silly. Baseball was the most popular sport in Japan, and of course everybody knew what the uniform looked like, or so I thought. Now I understood why so many books and magazines cluttered the studio. They were research materials. I wondered if I could draw anything from memory. The only consolation was that Tokida's drawing wasn't much better than mine.

"Kiyoi, watch Tokida and give him a hand," said Sensei.

Tokida moved over so I could sit next to him and watch what he was doing. With a brush he inked in the night skies, patterns on kimonos, hairdos — putting small touches here and there, giving life to the line drawings. When each frame was completed and the pencil lines erased, the finished drawings stood out against the sleek creamy paper. They were beautiful even before they were tinted with watercolor.

"Here, do this one," said Tokida casually, and gave me a board and a brush. "Fill in the large spots, like this man's coat. Always start from the top and work from left to right so you won't smudge the ink. And put a piece of paper under your hand so you won't grease up the board."

This was more frightening than drawing the horse yesterday. The master was actually going to let me work on his drawings. He and Tokida acted as though I'd been working with them for a long time. I felt like I was going into a duel with a real sword, without having gone through any training with a bamboo stick. Timidly, with a shaky hand, I started at a safe place — in the middle of a blank area — and worked outward. As I went near the edges, I unconsciously grasped the brush harder with each stroke, but the brush had a way of wandering off by itself, right over the outlines. I was making a mess.

"Don't worry about it; keep going," Tokida encouraged me.

"But I've ruined it," I said, nearly in tears.

"That's nothing," said Sensei. "You should have seen Tokida when he started; he has the shakiest hand I've ever seen. Too much smoking. He'll show you what to do."

Tokida dipped a new brush into a jar of thick white paint and went over the mess I'd made.

"All you have to do is cover it up with white and the camera won't pick it up," he told me.

"What do you mean?"

"They photograph these drawings to make the printing plates."

What a relief! The drawing didn't have to be discarded. Now that I knew a dab of white paint would hide all my mistakes, I went to work with a renewed spirit. I ran the brush along the straight lines of the frame borders and found that I had more control when I painted with swift strokes.

"Very good, Kiyoi," said Sensei. "You used something sharp in the brush just now, like the edge of a knife. The brush is many things. Remember that edge."

He was right. There *was* something sharp in the brush, and I could cut a straight or curved line with a quick turn of my wrist. And the amount of ink on the brush had a lot to do with what you could do with it. I felt as if I was learning calligraphy all over again.

After I was through inking the piece, Tokida showed me how to accent rounded objects — wheels, balls, hairdos and such — to give them a sense of volume. It was thrilling to see a flat line drawing suddenly become three-dimensional by putting in the highlights. At first I couldn't handle the brush well enough to use the white of the paper for the highlights, so I had to put them in with white paint, but after a while I got carried away and began to put in two or three highlights on a single object.

"The sun, the sun, Kiyoi," said Sensei. "One sun, one shadow, one highlight."

"Yes, sir."

At noon Sensei sent me to a restaurant to order our lunch.

"Noro Shinpei's place?" asked the woman who looked like the owner's wife.

"Yes, we'd like three bowls of noodles with shrimp, please."

"We haven't seen you before, have we?"

"No, I'm new."

"What happened to Tokida-san?"

"He's working with Sensei. I'm the new pupil."

"What, another one?" The woman looked me up and down. "But you seem so young. You must be awfully good to be his student."

Even the owner came out of the kitchen to inspect me. It was wonderful to have a famous master.

❖ ❖ ❖

The reporter came early. He was a fat man by the name of Kato, about twenty-five years old. He talked a lot, mostly about books which he produced out of his bulging briefcase. He was paid that day, he said, and the first thing he did was go to his bookdealer, settle the old account, and buy more books on credit. I thought it was amusing that a fat man would see his bookdealer before seeing his grocer.

When Sensei was finished with the boards we all went out for a break. I was as tall as Sensei, and for once I felt proud of my height. Tokida wore an old high school cap, and his wooden clogs gave him an extra three inches or so, but even then we walked shoulder to shoulder. Mr. Kato looked like a schoolboy walking next to us.

The cafe across the street from the train station was empty. The two waitresses and the owner greeted us as if we were a lordly procession, bowing and calling our master "Sensei" as Tokida and I did. So did Mr. Kato. I liked all the attention and looked at Tokida, but it was hard to tell what he was thinking. He was smoking one cigarette after another, drawing away in his sketchbook.

"My friends will sample your excellent coffee, and I'll have the usual," Sensei said to one of the waitresses.

"Have a sip." He pushed the tall silver mug in front of me when she brought it. I sucked on the straw and nearly burned the roof of my mouth. I'd never had hot orange juice before.

"Kiyoi has the cat's tongue." Sensei laughed. "Nothing hot for him. A pity, this being my own invention. Speaking of invention, do you realize that someone actually invented this?" Sensei lifted the straw.

"Someone with a case of mumps, I suppose," said Mr. Kato.

"Lockjaw is more likely. Who but the French would think of such a thing? All those Parisians in outdoor cafes sipping their drinks in an air thick with horse dung. And so the straw. The proper etiquette is to drink from the bottom up and leave the top layer untouched. That's what I call sophistication."

"Another one of your stories," said Mr. Kato.

"I thought you were well-read, Kato. Most of the so-called high fashion originated in such trivia. Take the high collar, for example . . ."

"That I know, a boil on Edward's neck. Or was it King George?" said the reporter. "Talking to a cartoonist is like talking to an encyclopedia."

"Full of useless information," Sensei agreed.

"Where is our coffee?" asked Mr. Kato as he looked at his watch.

"They're grinding the mocha beans for you. It'll be here any minute, a special treat for my friends and associates," replied Sensei.

"But I must be leaving in a few minutes."

"What's the hurry?"

"I have another appointment, and then I have a rendezvous at five-thirty."

"I thought you got married last year."

"I did, but we're trying to keep it fresh, you see, as fresh as a new romance. Once a month, on my payday, we meet somewhere after work, and pretend we're out for the first time. You must try it sometime, Sensei." Mr. Kato gave Sensei a sly grin. I turned to Tokida and saw him reaching for another cigarette.

"Wisdom of the newlywed," Sensei said.

"Well, one never knows what's going to happen when the first baby arrives. Keep it fresh as long as you can is what I say. I really must be going now, gentlemen."

"By the way, Kato, we're going to be moving to a new place," said Sensei. "It got a little cramped this morning, the three of us trying to work on that desk of mine. Now that I have Kiyoi, we need more space, to accommodate his long legs if nothing else."

"Not again, Sensei. The last time I couldn't find you for a month. My editor-in-chief blames me for everything, even for your disappearances. Please, Sensei, I don't want to lose my job quite yet. There's a chance of my being promoted, so please let me know as soon as you move. Good meeting you, Kiyoi-san. I'll see you next week." Mr. Kato gulped down the strong coffee and hurried out.

"Are we really moving, Sensei?" Tokida looked up from his sketchbook.

"It's time, Tokida. There's an inn I like in Takata-no-Baba."

"Why an inn?" asked Tokida. "Why can't you rent a studio somewhere?"

"I'm partial to inns. No leases, no deposits, and you can leave anytime you want. And most important, the room service."

"Do you move often?" I asked.

"Often enough, though I haven't moved since Tokida's been with me."

"I was lucky I found you yesterday then," I said.

"Kiyoi, I have a feeling you would've tracked me down no matter where I went. Thanks to Tokida's notoriety I've been getting more calls lately. And those reporters, all they can think about is deadlines, deadlines."

"That reporter is a strange fellow," said Tokida, "going out on a date with his own wife."

"What's wrong with that?"

"It's silly. Don't you think so, Sensei? I mean why did he get married in the first place if he has to date his own wife?"

Sensei laughed. "He's what they call a romantic, Tokida."

Tokida and I had another cup of coffee, then the three of us walked to Sensei's house. Sensei's wife was a young Kyushu woman, and her familiar accent made me like her immediately. Her name was Masako, same as my mother's. She and Sensei had two children, a girl about five and a boy about three. I kept looking at the children, and suddenly realized they looked very much like the children Sensei drew in his strips.

"So you're Kiyoi-san." Mrs. Noro gave me a smile. It was strange to see a famous cartoonist married, with children, and leading a normal life like anybody else.

Mrs. Noro invited us to stay for dinner but I declined. I wanted to be alone to think about all the things that had happened to me that day. Tokida said he had to return to the studio to finish some drawings. He probably felt that Sensei needed a quiet evening with his family and didn't want to get in the way.

FOUR

❖ ❖ ❖ ❖ ❖

On Wednesday Sensei gave notice to move, and by Friday we were finished with all the work, a full week ahead of schedule.

"If it weren't for you, Kiyoi, I'd be holed up here through the night," Sensei said. Though I knew he was exaggerating, his compliment pleased me. I was glad Tokida didn't hear him.

When Sensei left to spend the weekend with his family, Tokida and I spread out the finished boards on the long desk. There was something magical about the oversized artwork. We could see where Sensei's hand had quivered ever so slightly, where the pen had skipped, blotches of color where the brush had hesitated — things one would never notice on the printed page.

"Let's sign our names on them," said Tokida.

"We can't do that," I said in alarm.

"Why not? They don't have to be obvious." And he made a tiny mark in the middle of a bushy tree, another in a kimono pattern.

"You don't think Sensei will notice?"

23

"Well, look at it. If you didn't know I'd done it, could you tell my name was there?"

I had to admit I could not.

"Sensei never looks at them after they're printed anyway."

"How about putting in some birds in the sky then?" I said.

"Sure, but make them small."

We sat there a long time putting our coded names on practically every frame, beautifying the landscapes with birds and bugs and suspicious-looking flowers.

"When will this come out?" I asked, suddenly eager to see my work in print for the first time.

"In a couple of weeks. Let's go to that cafe."

"The hot orange juice place?"

"The same one. Nice waitresses. I'll buy you a cup of coffee."

We put away the boards, locked up the studio, and strolled to the cafe. I had a thick sketchbook now, like Tokida's, and I felt like I was wearing the badge of an artist. The two waitresses and the owner greeted us as before; they even remembered our names. We sat down by the window and ordered coffee, and when Tokida put a cigarette in his mouth, one of the waitresses struck a match to light it. I almost felt like smoking myself.

"Why does Sensei make fun of the police?" I asked.

"He's always making fun of them," said Tokida. "He used to be a political cartoonist and the police were always after him during the war. Do you know he's also a writer?"

I nodded. I had read many of his science fiction stories, but I didn't know he had been a political cartoonist.

"Did Sensei make up his pen name during the war, then?"

"Probably. He was doing drawings the police didn't like, so he had to go underground. That's why he never served in the army. They would've killed him."

"Tell me how you got to be Sensei's pupil."

"Don't you read the papers?"

"I read some of the things they said about you," I admitted. "Did you really walk all the way from Osaka?"

"That was the only way I could get here; I had no money. The

24

first time I ran away I got caught. I'd walked for ten days and got as far as Hakone, by Mount Fuji. A truck driver felt sorry for me and gave me a lift into Tokyo. The only problem was that he dropped me off at a police station. He thought the police would help me."

"What did they do to you?"

"They kept me up all night and asked me questions. They wanted to know where I'd been, what I'd stolen, things like that. Then they took my knife away. So I told them stories. I told them my old man was poor, Ma had cancer, and I started to cry because I started to believe the stories I was telling them. It didn't fool them, though. They wanted to know why I walked all the way from Osaka carrying a knife. They thought I was after somebody, so I told them the truth. I told them I'd come to Tokyo to be a cartoonist. They thought I was crazy. Why couldn't I be a cartoonist in Osaka, they asked me. I told them there weren't great cartoonists in Osaka, and besides Pa wouldn't let me, so they sent me home, with an escort."

"Did they handcuff you?"

"No, but they would have if I'd tried to run."

"What happened at home?"

"My old man beat me, and kicked me with his clogs. I thought he was going to kill me. That's when I lopped off my finger," he said, casually lifting his left hand to show me the missing finger. I grasped my hand under the table.

"It still hurts in damp weather," he said.

"Why did you want to hurt yourself like that?"

"I was so mad, I just took an axe and did it."

"But you could've lopped off your hand!"

"I didn't care. I didn't care if I lopped off my whole arm."

"Did your father see you do it?"

"I did it right in front of him. That shut him up. He was drunk as usual, and probably thought I was going to use the axe on him, and he stopped raving. He knew I always carried a knife. I used to be a *yakuza*," Tokida said, almost proudly, and sat back to see how I'd react. I felt a chill. A *yakuza* is a hoodlum who swears a lifetime

25

brotherhood with a group of gangsters who think nothing of murdering people with samurai swords.

"So what happened the second time you ran away?" I asked, not wanting to hear about his *yakuza* days.

"I made sure I wasn't going to get caught," he said. "I walked during the night and hid during the day."

"Did you have money?"

"Of course not. I dug up potatoes and turnips and ate them raw. You'd be amazed what you can live on when you have to."

"What did you do once you got to Tokyo?"

"First I went to a newspaper publisher's office to find out where Sensei lived. A couple of reporters started asking me questions, and for a while I thought they were going to turn me over to the police. Then they tried to reach Sensei but no one knew where his studio was. Like Sensei said, he was constantly moving in those days. Anyway, they gave me food and pumped me for information, and the next day they did that front-page story about me."

"I know, I read it."

"Well, around noon that day this wild-looking man came into the office. He looked weird in that long kimono of his; nobody wears something like that anymore. And those clogs. I couldn't believe it when he said he was Noro Shinpei; he's so famous I thought he'd be an old man. Do you know what he said to me? He said if *he* was good enough for me he'd be glad to take me on. Imagine that."

"He saved you," I said, and realized what a stupid thing I'd said. "What do you think would've happened if Sensei hadn't come?" I asked quickly.

"I thought about killing myself before my old man got to me," he said coolly, drawing on his cigarette.

"Somebody would've helped you. If it wasn't Sensei, it would've been somebody else."

"Maybe, but I doubt it." Tokida opened his sketchbook and began to draw me from across the table. "And what about you?" he asked. "That took a lot of nerve, walking in on Sensei like that."

"Well, for one thing I read about you in the paper. That was

26

where I got Sensei's address. I cut out the article and saved it. You don't know how many times I read it. I always thought I was the only one who wanted to be a cartoonist."

"If you come from a rich family, cartooning is not supposed to be respectable. But who cares? If you really want to do something, you should do it no matter what. You know why you want to be a cartoonist?"

"I'm not sure," I said. "Sensei asked me that too. All I ever wanted to do was to draw cartoons. I think it's good to make people laugh. And everybody reads comics."

"That's right," agreed Tokida. "Cartooning is an art, like painting or calligraphy or anything else, but that's only for you and me. I couldn't even talk about comic books in front of my old man, and he's not the type to worry about being respectable — far from it. Your pa is rich, right?"

"No, he isn't really," I lied.

"All right, respectable then. And you say he doesn't care if you become a cartoonist?"

"I never told him. I never told anybody, but don't tell Sensei. My father would have a fit if he found out what I was doing; I told him I was taking painting lessons. He thinks it's a nice hobby."

"Well, sooner or later you'll have to tell him. And then what?"

"Maybe I'll run away like you did. Would you like to see a movie?" I changed the subject.

"Yes, sure, it's early," he agreed.

We left the cafe and walked across the street to the train station. I was glad Tokida didn't ask me any more questions about my family.

FIVE

❖ ❖ ❖ ❖ ❖

The three-room suite in the old inn at the edge of the residential district in Tokyo called Takata-no-Baba was the sort of old mansion I had imagined when I first went to look for Sensei. Tokida slept in one of the smaller rooms, and Sensei in the other whenever he couldn't go home because of a deadline rush. We worked in the spacious twelve-mat room on the second floor that looked out onto a traditional garden with pines and Japanese apricots and maples, and a carp pond with a stone bridge over it. The big tiled tub in the bathhouse was filled with hot water all hours of the day, and food could be ordered from the kitchen almost anytime.

On our first day there, Tokida and I hopped over the balcony railing and went scuttling barefoot over the waves of roofing tiles. The highest point on the roof was almost four stories high, and the clothes-drying platform stood on top of that.

"What a place to fly a kite," said Tokida, lighting a cigarette. Perched on the platform, we stood taller than anything in the neighborhood. We felt like a couple of young warlords looking over our domain.

"Look at those people down there," he said. "They look like little bugs."

He hopped off the platform and went down to the ridge of the main roof. "Let's have some fun," he said, hurling a small piece of mortar down onto the street below.

"Duck, you fool, do you want us to get caught?" he hissed at me. I crouched next to him.

"It's your turn." He handed me a clump of dirt. I hesitated.

"Go on, throw it; you're not going to kill anybody."

I tossed the dirt ball halfheartedly over the ridge.

"Coward! You didn't throw it hard enough. Take a bigger piece, here, like this," he said, aiming a walnut-sized dirt ball at a man walking a dog. We followed the missile with our eyes and ducked as soon as it shattered on the sidewalk, missing both the man and his dog.

"It's your turn," said Tokida and handed me a big clump of dirt. I threw it down toward the street as hard as I could.

"Ouch!" a voice shouted.

We didn't dare stick our heads out. I crouched next to Tokida, killing my breath. Tokida was holding his mouth with both hands.

"You . . . you . . . ," he said between muffled laughter. "You're a pretty good shot."

"I wasn't even aiming at anybody," I whispered.

"That's why you're a good shot."

After a while we slowly slid down the roof like crabs and into the safety of our room, where we howled with laughter.

"Hey, what's going on?" said Sensei, standing behind us in the doorway. We sat up straight, but when we saw him we roared. There he was, in his usual kimono, hugging a life-sized plaster statue of a naked woman.

"I'm glad you find her amusing, but not for long, I assure you. She's going to give you two some pain, a lot of grief, I hope. Meet Venus de Milo," he announced and set the statue on the floor.

"We were telling jokes, Sensei," said Tokida, wiping his tears. "Did you know Kiyoi is a good shot?"

I glared at him.

"I bet. Up to no good, I'm sure. Are you two ready for some work?"

"Yes, sir," we said eagerly.

"Good. If we finish the first two pages I'll treat you to an extraordinary meal."

"Where?" asked Tokida.

"A high-class restaurant. Tokida, see if you have a pair of socks with no holes in them. They serve live loaches in a shallow pan. Have you ever tasted them, Kiyoi?"

I shook my head.

"You have a treat coming. They take a pan, put a little water in it, and then set a block of bean cake in the middle, with the fish swimming all around the cake. Then they put the pan over a fire right on your table, and as the water begins to get hot, the fish begin to look for a cold place, which is the bean cake, of course, and they swim into it. Thus the fish get cooked in this neat package. A delightful dish."

"That's barbaric!" I cried. "I never heard of such a thing."

"Kiyoi, barbarism is a word unknown in gastronomy. Tokida, do you have a pair of shoes?"

"Just my tennis shoes, Sensei."

"Remind me to get you a pair."

"You must have been paid today." Tokida grinned.

"How did you guess?" Sensei said and went to his room to change.

"Good thing it wasn't Sensei you hit," said Tokida, throwing an eraser at me. I ducked and began to laugh again.

"All right, a little work," said Sensei, sitting down at the low table in a light kimono the inn had provided. He lit a cigarette and was silent for a while. Tokida and I watched the great man think.

"Wasn't it Napoleon who said that the word 'impossible' had no place in his dictionary?" asked Sensei.

"Yes," I said.

"That's why it was cheap," said Tokida.

"Think of something that's impossible to do."

"There's no medicine to cure a fool," said Tokida, quoting an old saying.

"Not bad, but something less tragic."

"You can't fish where there's no water," I said, paraphrasing another old saying.

"Very good, but too philosophical. Give me something more mundane."

"I know," I exclaimed. "You can't lick your own elbow."

Immediately Sensei rolled up his sleeve and tried to reach his elbow with his tongue.

"You're quite right. Tokida, see if you can do it."

So the three of us sat there, trying to shove our elbows toward our mouths.

"That's it! Tokida, line up the boards."

Quickly he began to lay out a story about Napoleon in Japan looking for something impossible to do.

"How do you come up with your ideas?" I asked.

"You were the one who gave me the idea."

"Do you always know beforehand what's going to happen in the next installment?"

"Never. Something always happens. I'm not saying it just happens out of nowhere. Something like your idea would get my mind going and the story unfolds itself. Pay attention to all that goes on around you. Remember, memory is the most important asset to an artist. What we call imagination is rearrangement of memory. You cannot imagine without memory. Then there's intuition. If you pay attention, in the end your intuition will come into play; you have to learn to trust your intuition."

"Do we all have intuition?" asked Tokida.

"No question. Some more than others, but we all have it."

"But how can you come up with all your ideas time after time," I persisted.

"By paying attention. If I didn't pay attention to what you said, I'd still be struggling with Napoleon."

"But you asked us for the idea in the first place," Tokida pointed out.

"Quite right, Tokida. An old Chinese sage said that you don't ask a question unless you're near the answer."

Is that true? I wondered. And if true, there had to be an answer to every question. Did it mean every time I questioned something the answer was just around the corner? And since I was asking *that*, the answer must have been within my grasp. It didn't seem possible. Besides, it was all too confusing. I would have to think about it later, when I was alone.

Sensei took us to the Ginza for our night out. We walked the neon-bright boulevards and back alleys with thousands of office workers on their way home from work. The narrow streets were crammed with eating and drinking places, reeking of roasting fowl and meats. The cafe hostesses stood in front of doorways and beckoned us inside. They looked harsh and beautiful under the blinking colored lights.

Sensei led us into a restaurant with a small entrance in front. We removed our shoes on the porch and a woman attendant put them in a shoe box and ushered us upstairs. The restaurant was one huge room. People sat around low tables and the waitresses in kimonos raced around them, carrying stacks of dishes, steaming pans of fish and broth, sake and beer, and the tea things.

"You can relax, Kiyoi, this is not the loach place," said Sensei as we sat on the floor. "I felt daring tonight, so I decided to live dangerously. *Fugu* is the specialty of this house."

"Blowfish?" asked Tokida.

"Have you ever had it?"

We shook our heads.

"It's a great delicacy, a classic dish that requires a good deal of skill to prepare."

"It's poisonous," I said.

"The glands are lethal, but the flesh is delicious."

"People can die eating it," said Tokida.

"Therein lies the titillation. Come, where's your sense of adventure? I told you I was feeling daring tonight. The chef here is a good friend of mine. To my knowledge he hasn't killed anyone yet.''

"A wise man avoids danger," said Tokida.

"So said Confucius. I say what does a vegetarian know?''

"Was Confucius a vegetarian?'' I asked innocently.

"He who refrains from eating a delicate fish is a vegetarian. But order anything you wish. I recommend either a crab or a shrimp dish.''

"I'm going to try the *fugu*," announced Tokida.

"So will I," I said.

"That's more like it. Here, this will give you courage." He offered us hot sake.

By the time our waitress brought our food, Tokida's face had turned bright red.

"Kiyoi is going to be a strong drinker," commented Sensei, reddening around his eyes. Unlike Tokida's, my face didn't change color with sake.

The deadly fish came in a clear broth and tasted like any ordinary fish, like red snapper or halibut. After all the buildup it was a disappointment.

SIX

❖ ❖ ❖ ❖ ❖

The two weeks went by quickly.

On the last Saturday before school began I went to the inn in the midmorning. The place was empty. I called Tokida's name several times before I heard a muffled sound from his room. As I slid open the door I saw him sitting cross-legged in the middle of the floor, facing the *shoji* screen. For a moment I thought he was meditating. Then he turned his head.

His whole face was covered with streaks of blood!

"What did you do to yourself!" I shouted at him, horrified.

Tokida didn't answer. He was holding a small pocket mirror in one hand and a naked razor in the other.

"What are you doing!" I shouted again.

"Pimples. Stupid pimples. I pinch them and squash them and they keep coming back, so I decided to cut them off."

"You're crazy! Your face is going to be scarred for good!"

"So what? Why should you care? You don't have pimples."

"Stop it, right now! Stop cutting yourself!"

Tokida squinted severely at me with his nearsighted eyes. Blood oozed on his face like beads of sweat. I felt nauseated looking at him. He took a crumpled handkerchief out of his pocket and covered his face with it. In an instant the white cloth was soaked.

"I'll get you some iodine."

"Don't bother. Sit down."

"But your face is going to get infected."

"It's all right, I tell you. Come and sit."

I sat down, facing him. He kept wiping his face and after a while the bleeding stopped. His face was crosshatched with razor slits. He put his glasses on and smiled.

"See this?" He pointed at the gas outlet. "I wonder how long it'll take to kill me. They say it's the best way to commit suicide. You don't feel a thing. You just go to sleep and never wake up."

Then he lay down on the floor, stuck his face right up against the outlet, and turned the gas full blast. Thinking it was a joke, I sat still and said nothing, waiting for him to turn the gas off. Soon the small room was filled with the heavy smell of rat poison. Tokida lay perfectly still and showed no sign of turning the gas off. I knew he was testing me, but I didn't know how to react to it. The steady hissing of the gas seemed very loud now, and Tokida lay there like a dead man. I panicked. I bolted out of the room, calling frantically for Sensei. I rushed down the staircase and out into the garden in my stocking feet, and for no reason ran around the carp pond. Then I charged into the bathhouse. No one in sight. Like a wild man I ran around the inn. No one. Not even the old innkeeper.

I rushed back to Tokida's room. The smell was unbearable now. Holding my breath, I lunged at the gas outlet and turned it off. Tokida lay very still, his eyes closed. An awful thought crossed my mind: It's too late. I shook him violently.

"Wha — what happened?" he stirred and whispered in a stupor. I rushed to the *shoji* screen, jerked it open, and spat out the air in my lungs.

"Idiot!" I shouted. "You ass!"

Seeing that he was alive, I let out my rage. "So your old man's a drunk! So you had to walk three hundred miles! So your face is lousy with pimples! So you think you're somebody special! You're an idiot!"

"Quit screaming. My head is splitting."

"Good! I hope your head cracks!"

"Hey, take it easy. I was only experimenting. Go see if you can find some pills. Look in Sensei's room. . . . My head . . ."

"If you want to experiment, do it when there's no one around," I said and went to look for the pills.

When I returned with a glass of water and four aspirin tablets, Tokida sat up and gave me a sheepish grin.

"Let's go eat. I'll buy you a bowl of noodles," he said, popping the pills in his mouth.

My knees were shaking and I felt sick to my stomach, but I was so relieved that Tokida was alive I felt weightless. But I kept scowling to show him how angry I was. After a while we staggered out to a small restaurant. It was good to be out and breathing fresh air. We ate our lunch in silence, avoiding each other's eyes. His face was a mess.

"How's your head?" I asked finally.

"Almost back to normal." He gave me a weak smile.

"Why don't we go over to my place?"

"You still mad at me?"

"No. Do you want to come?"

"I don't want to see anybody."

"Nobody's home. There won't be anybody to admire your face."

"Is it that bad?"

"A little makeup would help. How about it, Tokida? We're all caught up with work and my school doesn't start till next week. It would be good if you could come today."

"You're sure nobody's going to be home?"

"I promise."

"Aw, all right." He sounded as if he were doing me a favor, but that was his way.

The district where I lived had been hit hard in the war, and most of the shabby houses had been built helter-skelter four or five years ago. The unpaved roads and alleys turned into a soupy mess after a good rain. Tokida seemed surprised — even a little pleased — to see that I lived in such a neighborhood.

My room seemed starker than usual. The somber light through the milky windowpane made the place look like a room in a Zen monastery. Even the dull aluminum kettle on the hot plate seemed bright in the shadowy light. There wasn't even a radio, and the old alarm clock ticked loudly on the writing desk.

"This is it, my eel's bed." I waved my arm around.

"I don't believe it," Tokida said in amazement. He looked around as if to find more rooms hidden somewhere. "Are your ma and pa dead? I mean, who takes care of you?"

"I'm not an orphan, if that's what you're wondering. Why don't we sit down. How about a cup of tea?"

"Sure. So who takes care of you?" He seemed bewildered. I was enjoying myself.

"I do. Well, my mother gives me money to live on. My parents are divorced."

"Divorced? I never heard of such a thing. Nobody gets a divorce."

"I know. I never told anybody. No one at my school knows about it."

"Do they know you live alone?"

"Of course not. I've never brought anybody home before."

"All right, I'm honored. But where are they? Your parents."

"Mother has a small shop in Yokohama — she sells cosmetics. And my father is in Kyushu. We moved there after the war because our house was burned down in the war, and my father couldn't find work in Tokyo. He's remarried and has a family. My grandmother is supposed to be in charge of me; she has a house here in Tokyo. I lived with her until about a year ago, but we didn't get along too well, so she rented this place for me. Are you interested in all this?"

"Sure, but why didn't you tell me before?"

"I didn't want Sensei to know."

"Let me tell you, Kiyoi, you can tell Sensei anything."

"That's because you know him better than I do. I lied to him about my parents because I didn't think he'd take me on if he knew I didn't have my parents' permission. And who's ever heard of someone my age living alone? They'd probably throw me out of school if they found out I lived in a place like this."

"What do you mean a place like this? It's a fine place. And who cares anyway? Let them go to the dogs. You go to Aoyama, right? Sensei says it's a school for the rich. I hate those snobs. If you're smart enough to pass the entrance exam, why should they care where you live? Schools are a waste of time anyway. All I did in school was fight and draw cartoons. I like your place."

"I do too. Sometimes, though, I wake up in the morning and I don't know where I am. You know that feeling? But I can read and draw all I want."

"You're lucky to have a place of your own. What does your old man do?"

"He sells pearls."

"He's rich then. Did you say you were born in Yokohama?"

"Yes, but during the war, when the B-29's started to bomb us, Mother and I went to live with her people in Yamaguchi. Father stayed behind to earn money. He was working in Tokyo."

"Yamaguchi? That's just the other side of Hiroshima, isn't it?"

"That's right. It's only an hour's ride on a train."

"You remember the bomb?"

"I remember a lot of it. I was eight when it happened. There were mountains all around us so we didn't see the flash, but we felt it. It was like a big earthquake; I thought our house was going to fall down. Mother read the paper in the afternoon and said an atomic bomb had been dropped in Hiroshima. And you know, nobody knew what that was."

"I remember that," said Tokida. "I must have been about eleven. We didn't know what it was either. Nobody knew."

"My cousin used to work in Hiroshima and we worried about her, but she came home late in the afternoon. She was on a train full of people running away from the city. It was awful."

"Is she still alive?"

"Yes. She still has gravel and bits of glass in her skin. She used to make me feel them with my hand. And she has no hair left on her body. She smelled awful when she came home, with her skin all burned and blistered. She screamed and raved all night and two men had to keep her pinned down on the bed because she was begging for a sword. . . . The men yelled at me and Mother to hide all the knives and scissors and anything sharp so my cousin couldn't kill herself.

"Later, my cousin told me that after the explosion she had dragged her girl friend from the fallen building where they worked and they were stumbling around in fire and smoke. Her friend kept begging for water and finally my cousin found a burst water pipe and gave her some. She drank the water and died. So my cousin wouldn't touch water after that."

Tokida stared at me for some time.

"Didn't you hate the Americans?" he asked, almost in a hiss.

"I hated those B-29's, and do you remember those black Grummans that flew so low and sprayed machine gun bullets? It's funny, but I always thought Americans were airplanes. Stupid, isn't it? I never thought they were people."

I remembered the first time I saw American soldiers. The war had been over for only a few days, and Mother and I went to the seaport town of Sasebo to join Father. It was a long and terrible journey, but we were happy, eager to see Father after our long separation. As we got off the train we saw Americans all over the station. They were enormous. Most of them were sailors, and many of them had pistols strapped around their waists. When we passed them by they pointed at Mother and laughed. She was dressed like a peasant woman and they probably thought she looked ugly. They talked loudly, lighting cigarettes, and flicked the long butts on the platform. A couple of laborers in tattered clothes dived after them, and the Americans roared with laughter. I was ashamed for my countrymen, and the size of Americans frightened me.

"My father is a Korean," I said, suddenly deciding to tell Tokida everything.

"So?" He cocked his head as if he didn't understand what I was saying.

"Well, aren't you surprised?"

"Why should I be surprised? What difference does that make? He's your pa, isn't he?"

I was a little disappointed in his reaction. I expected him to react the way he had when I told him my parents were divorced.

"I never told this to anybody before," I said. "Mother's family disowned her for marrying my father. That's about the worst disgrace, you know, for a woman from a samurai family to marry a Korean."

"People are so stupid," sneered Tokida.

"Actually my grandmother was the one who disowned my mother, and now Mother supports her. It really makes me angry sometimes. Did you know that all Koreans were stateless during the war? I mean my father was a man without a country. The military police thought he was a spy and tortured him. So now he wants to make a lot of money and emigrate to another country. He says the Japanese did some terrible things in China."

"They all did," said Tokida. "That's war. But it's funny you remember all that. While you were talking about your cousin, I was thinking about the day the war ended. We got ready to go to bed early that night, and all I could think about was that we didn't have to run out of the house every time we heard sirens. That's what Ma said, no more sirens. Then we heard somebody shouting outside. Ma and my little brother and I peeked out from behind the rain shutters to see what was going on. There was nobody out on the street except for this man sitting cross-legged in the middle of the intersection, ranting and raving about something. But he was so drunk we couldn't make out what he was saying. He'd shout something over and over between swigs till all of a sudden I realized he was quoting the emperor's surrender speech. After a while he started to sob out loud and nobody went to help him. It was terrible. Then he started yelling, 'Tomi, Tomi!' How weird, I thought. Tomi is Ma's name. And the next thing I knew, Ma yanked open the shutter and ran out of the house. It was Pa. We

40

couldn't believe it. He'd been a teetotaler all his life, and he's been a drunkard since. He always wanted me and my brother to die for our country, but now he didn't have anything to live for."

"I'm glad we weren't old enough to be soldiers," I said.

"So am I," Tokida agreed. We sipped our cold tea and said nothing for a while.

"Show me some of your drawings," said Tokida.

"I don't want to show them to you; they aren't any good."

"Don't be silly. Let me see them."

I showed him two sketchbooks I'd been using at school. It was terrible to have to sit and watch Tokida politely pore over every page. It was like having your diary read in front of you.

"They're all right, but you should draw more. You can fill up a pad like this in one afternoon. Have you ever done any life drawing?"

"What do you mean?"

"Nudes."

"No. Have you?"

"Sensei enrolled me in a night class. Tuesday and Thursday nights."

"Are the models really naked?"

"Of course. They're stark naked, pubic hair and all."

"Don't you get embarrassed?"

"At first I was, but you get used to it. It's like going to a public bathhouse, all natural; do you know what I mean? Sensei's probably going to make you take the class too. You'll see."

"But I'm not ready yet."

"You've got to start sometime."

"Yes, I suppose so," I agreed. The idea of drawing a naked woman excited me, but I didn't want Tokida to know it.

"Would you like a sip of this?" I brought out the bottle of port wine.

"You drink this stuff?" he asked suspiciously.

"I have a capful now and then. My next-door neighbor brought it over the other night, to improve my circulation, he told me."

"Sure, I'll have a sip. What does your neighbor do?"

"He's studying literature. He also has a black belt in karate."

"Is he good?" Tokida asked with interest.

"I've never watched him, but anyone who has a second-degree belt must be deadly."

We each drank a capful of the cheap wine.

"This is good," Tokida said. I poured him another drink.

"Are you going back to the inn for supper?" I asked.

"No, this is my night off, and Sensei went home for the weekend. He said for us to visit him anytime, but I don't want to bother him."

"No, let's not. How about some curried rice? I know a good place in Shibuya, only eighty yen."

"How's my face now?"

"Your face is fine. It's a dark place so no one will notice."

"Let's go." Tokida stood up and stretched his arms. "How about letting me borrow your bike sometime?"

"Take it anytime you want. I hardly ever use it."

SEVEN

❖❖❖❖❖

It was hard going back to school. I was never a good student, and studying seemed more boring than ever. At times I was convinced there were more teachers at my school than students, and they loaded us down with homework. I didn't know how the other students managed; most of them seemed happy and mindless. I didn't have a close friend and never shared my thoughts with anybody.

I was the tallest boy in my grade, and that didn't make things easy for me. I always sat in the back of classrooms, trying not to be too noticeable, but that didn't stop the teachers from calling me frequently to translate passages into English, or name some obscure historical names and dates. They always caught me by surprise. I had to stand up to give my answers, and the whole class would turn to watch me make a fool of myself. Then there were the morning assemblies where we had to sit in the cold auditorium and listen to moral stories and meditate. I hated school.

Time passed slowly. I was worried about breaking the news of my apprenticeship to Mother, and worse still to Grandmother. As it was, I was near the bottom of my class, and there was no way I could hide my grades from Grandmother. My school had a cruel way of announcing our grades. What they did was to invite all the parents to school after each midterm examination to inspect the exam papers themselves — not only the papers of their children, but anybody else's they chose to see. And being my guardian, Grandmother saw my grades even before I did. What would she say if she found out I was studying to be a cartoonist? The worst thing she could do was to make me give up my apartment, and that was unthinkable.

School dragged on.

❖ ❖ ❖

Sensei did enroll me in the life drawing class, and I was glad of Tokida's company on my first night there.

The class began at seven, but we arrived there half an hour early. The studio was in a big building with a pointed roof that had a skylight on one side. It was modern and European-looking, and seemed out of place among the Japanese-style houses.

Inside, the studio was like a stage set, with a platform in the center and chairs all around. A potbelly stove was roaring in the corner, though it wasn't a cold night, and three spotlights cast pools of light on the platform. Some serious-looking adults, mostly men, stood in silhouette near the platform. They talked in soft whispers, and the blue smoke from their cigarettes rose in coils, catching the spotlights. They were talking to a young woman in a dark robe, sitting limp on a chair. Her hair was tied in a ponytail so her face was fully exposed. She wasn't especially pretty. She had on a pair of house slippers, and half hidden by the felt of the slippers I saw the naked toes and the bare skin of her ankle.

"Is she the model?" I whispered to Tokida.

"I've drawn her a couple of times," he said casually. "She's one of the better ones."

My heart began to beat fast in anticipation. In a few minutes I would be looking at her without any clothes. I asked Tokida where the toilet was and he nodded toward the back of the studio. Whenever I was nervous I had to run to a toilet, like a little dog.

"We'd better take our seats," said Tokida when I came out.

"Can we sit in the back? I don't want to sit by the platform," I said.

Tokida gave me an odd look, a kind of leer, then shook his head and chuckled.

"All right, let's start," said a man with a beret cocked on his head. The crowd broke up and took seats around the platform. The young woman put out her cigarette, stood up, and let her robe fall on the chair. I was taken by surprise. She was stark naked. Somehow, I had expected her to disrobe gradually, underwear and all, but there she was, with nothing on, looking as cool as anything. Then she shook off her slippers and stepped onto the platform. She put her hands on her hips, with her legs slightly parted, and turned her head a little to the side and stared straight ahead. Her armpits had been shaven clean, like women in Western movies. It was impossible to tell what she was thinking, but that was just as well — I was busy with my own thoughts. The potbelly stove behind me felt like an open furnace. I was glad of the large sketchbook I'd brought, and held it in front of me to cover my groin.

"Sit down somewhere and start drawing," Tokida hissed in my ear. I couldn't believe his nonchalance. First he polished his glasses, slowly, then he took out a package of cigarettes, took one out, and tapped it against his drawing pad. He was always tapping his cigarettes, and for once it got on my nerves; I wanted to kick him in his shin. Finally he opened his sketchbook to a clean page and began to draw. I couldn't bring myself to look at the model, so I watched Tokida to see what he was doing. He drew the woman's head at the top of the page. I did the same.

I knew I was acting like an idiot, but couldn't help myself. I had seen naked women before, mostly in public baths, hot spring resorts and such, where people bathe together. But this was different. No matter what Tokida said, staring at a grown, naked woman on a platform wasn't natural. It was exciting. I began to think

45

perhaps I should become a painter so I could have models in my studio. The thought made my ears hot.

There was a woman in the group in her forties who looked like a hawk, with piercing eyes and hair pulled straight back on her skull. And just as I wondered how she felt about looking at a naked woman, she barked at the model for not holding her pose. The woman's voice was rough, and her rudeness surprised me. One would've thought she was drawing a horse.

During the breaks the model walked around, looking at everyone's drawings. It must have been a strange experience for her to see how people saw her. I held my sketchbook tightly on my lap, with the cover closed. But Tokida seemed cool and confident, leaving his drawing on his chair for everyone to see, and of course everybody stopped to look at it. I admit his drawing was the best, and he knew it.

"How are you doing?" Tokida asked me. He was being smug, but I felt too unnerved even to ask him a question.

"Don't try to draw her hands and feet. Forget the face, just worry about the outline and volume," he suggested. He sounded as if he were drawing a house or a car.

After three hours of drawing I did get used to looking at the model without feeling embarrassed.

For the last half hour the model did a series of five-minute poses and we had to draw quickly. I didn't have the time to worry about the hands and toes, and drew frantically. I'd never drawn so hard in my life, and was exhausted when we left the studio.

It was ten-thirty when we got off the train at Shibuya, from where I was to take a bus home. The neon lights were still blazing and the streets bustled with taxis and people who didn't seem to know how late it was. Tokyo hardly ever sleeps, and that was one of the things I was beginning to like about the city.

"How about a cup of coffee?" asked Tokida.

"It's late," I said. "And coffee keeps me up all night."

"Then have tea or something."

"All right, one cup then." I gave in reluctantly. We walked

among university students and drunks, the late shoppers and lovers strolling hand in hand. Suddenly I noticed something new in myself: I was looking at women in a way I'd never done before. Pretty faces, especially eyes, attracted me still, but I was beginning to see more. I stole quick glances at their kimonos, blouses, skirts, yet they no longer hid from me their breasts and hips and thighs. I felt hot inside.

"Look," said Tokida and grasped me by the arm. He led me to a shop window full of knives and daggers with exposed blades. He was pointing at a long switchblade knife with a bone handle.

"Have you ever seen one of those?" he asked me. I shook my head.

"They really work. A friend of mine used to have one back in Osaka. Let's go in and have a look."

"It's almost closing time, Tokida."

"It'll only be a minute. I've always wanted to see one," he said and marched inside.

The place was empty except for a tired-looking clerk sitting at the far end of the shop. Two walls were covered with knives and scissors and straightedge razors of all sizes. Tokida pretended to look at some shaving things, though he probably shaved twice a week at the most.

"Is there something I can show you?" the clerk asked politely.

"What kind of a straightedge would you recommend for a beginner?" asked Tokida.

"Well, of course the imported blades are superior to anything we make, but they're also quite expensive. I have some decent domestic blades, though. You don't seem like a person who has to shave every day," he said and took out several razors from under the counter. Tokida picked up one, opened the long blade and put its edge against his tongue.

"What are you doing?" I said in alarm.

"This is how you tell if a blade is sharp," he answered. "If it's really sharp you can taste it, a kind of sour taste. Isn't that right?"

"I've seen people do that, yes, but personally I find it a little

47

risky," the clerk said and pulled out a hair from his head and sliced it with a razor.

"That's really sharp," said Tokida, "but I think I'll stay with my old safety razor for now. My father gave it to me when I first started shaving, the kind that has a floating head on it. I think it's German."

"That's the best kind. You'll never see one of those anymore; that's a prewar item. You got yourself a real treasure."

Tokida surprised me. This was the first time I had heard him say "father" instead of the usual old man, or Pa.

"By the way, I noticed a switchblade in the window. Do you mind showing it to me?" Tokida finally came out with it.

"Of course, I have one right here. It's an interesting gadget," said the clerk, producing a knife in a slender case. Tokida held the knife in his right hand and stroked the catch release with his thumb. He turned it this way and that, admiring the smooth bone handle on the six-inch knife. Then suddenly he pressed down on the release and the slim blade fanned out in a flash, and locked itself in position with a loud click. I flinched involuntarily, as from a gunshot. The sleek blade looked like a surgical instrument, machinelike and sinister. It had none of the beauty of a classic suicide dagger. I saw excitement in Tokida's eyes as he folded the blade back and shot it out, again and again.

"You notice how the blade locks in place once it's all the way out," the clerk pointed out. "It's a nice safety feature."

"How much does a thing like this cost?" asked Tokida.

"That one goes for three thousand yen, and that's a bargain. But I'll tell you what. It's late, and you being my last customer I'll give it to you for two hundred less."

"Four hundred," bargained Tokida.

"Well, how about an even ten percent discount? Two thousand seven hundred."

"I don't have the money right now, but I will in a few days. Will you hold it for me?"

"Well," said the clerk, "what can I say? It's yours when you come back with the money."

48

"You won't forget about the discount, will you?"

"Don't worry, a bargain is a bargain," the clerk assured Tokida and put away the knife.

I thought Tokida's face was a bit flushed when we came out of the shop.

"You're not going to get that knife, are you?" I asked.

"Of course not. I only wanted to see if it really worked. It's beautiful, though."

"I think it's ugly, a gimmick, and it's probably made out of cheap steel. I bet you anything the spring will break after a while."

"But it's fast and small and light. You can carry it in your pocket and nobody will ever know it. Swish! When you're in a fight you don't have the time to fumble around. One time I thought a fight was coming on and I started to take off my glasses when this stiff hit me in the face. What if he had had a knife, I ask you."

"You're not going to carry a knife again, are you?"

"I just like knives, I guess. It would make me feel better if I had one of those on me."

"That's stupid. They say if you carry a weapon sooner or later you're going to use it."

"Don't worry. I only wanted to look at one, so forget it, will you?"

Somehow I felt uneasy; I'd never seen Tokida quite so excited, and the wild look in his eyes frightened me. We went into a cafe and ordered our drinks.

"Where did you learn to bargain like that?" I asked.

"How's that?"

"You know, when you talked that clerk out of three hundred yen."

"Oh, that. I should've gotten him to go down even lower. You never pay the price they tell you on anything. You're a fool if you do. Everything is marked up twenty, thirty percent."

"Why wasn't there an instructor tonight?" I asked, not wanting to talk about the knife anymore.

"What are you talking about?" said Tokida irritably.

"Nobody came around to instruct us how to draw."

"You mean *the* Master," he said sarcastically. "He comes around about once a month. He walks behind you, and most of the time he doesn't say a thing. You'd think he was a little god or something the way he struts around. Sometimes he says things like, 'Five years,' and walks away. And that's supposed to be a compliment. It means you show promise, and he'll talk to you again in five years. Who needs it? Talk to Sensei, he's the best."

"Are they any good? I mean the people who were drawing tonight."

"They're all amateurs; they don't know what they're doing. There's one fellow there, the one in a school uniform, who's flunked the entrance exam at Ueno three years in a row. Can you imagine anybody trying to get into some stupid art school for almost four years? The fool ought to know he's never going to make it. Schools are a waste of time, anyway. I'll tell you what most of them go there for. They go there twice a week to ogle at the models."

"What about the women then? What about that woman with the strange hairdo?"

"She's a dancer. Wants to know more about the body. She likes to walk around with paint smeared on her hands to show she's an artist."

"Do you think you'll ever change your mind and become a painter instead?"

"I don't think so. It's cartooning for me. Why do you ask? You think you might want to become a painter?"

"I don't know, but I'd like to learn to paint in oils. Wouldn't it be good to have a studio of your own, like the one we were in tonight?"

"So you can have naked models in there? Why don't you learn to draw first?" he sneered and crushed his empty cigarette package.

"Do you know how late the stores stay open?" he asked.

"You're still thinking about that stupid knife, aren't you?" I got back at him.

"Just curious. Let's get out of here."

We said good night at the station and went on our separate ways. I couldn't shake the feeling Tokida was holding out on me, that he had enough money to buy the switchblade and was going to go back for it.

EIGHT

❖ ❖ ❖ ❖ ❖

"Use your eyes," said Sensei, looking at my drawings of the nude. "Then your head, and then your hand. Right now you're using only your hand."

"Yes, sir."

"Pay attention to what you see. Concentrate. Look at the model, then look down on your paper and imagine how that picture inside your head is going to fit on the paper. Then draw the head first. That's how you determine where the rest of her body is going to go."

"What about hands and feet, Sensei? They're so hard to draw."

"For now think only about the large shapes. Think of the human body as something that's made up of a series of large shapes. Head is one shape, then the torso, the hip area, the thighs. Look at her as though she's made of bricks."

"Why do we have to draw nudes in the first place?"

"Because the human body is the most beautiful thing to draw. So much of cartooning is drawing figures, and because it's cartooning doesn't mean you can draw anatomically incorrect figures. A cartoonist has to be as fine a draftsman as a painter. And who knows, you may decide to become an illustrator or a painter someday. I consider drawing to be the most important thing I can teach you. One of these days I'm going to send you two to watch an autopsy so you'll understand how the body is put together."

"Prop me up when I start to faint, will you, Kiyoi," said Tokida. "You've seen an autopsy, Sensei?"

"It was a required course when I was in school."

"You went to an art school?" asked Tokida. He seemed surprised.

"I'll have you know that I even earned a degree from Ueno, that illustrious institution. It took me four years of schooling to discover that the world was run by a bunch of demented minds. You might say that political cartooning saved me from going insane."

So Sensei had been trained to become a painter, and the Ueno Academy was *the* art school in Japan. I was impressed.

"How long do I have to practice before I can draw hands and feet, Sensei?" I asked.

"A bad word, Kiyoi. Drawing is never a practice. You discover something new every time you draw. Discovery is what drawing is all about. Remember that."

"Yes, sir."

So whenever we would be caught up with our work, Tokida and I would draw Venus de Milo, using long sticks of charcoal and erasing with fresh bread. I had never used charcoal before and had a hard time working with it at first. The first few drawings turned out like some messy caricatures of a very black African, and one couldn't tell whether the subject was a man or a woman. But Tokida, who had been using charcoal for some time, was very good. His drawings had the look of the hard white plaster. I couldn't understand how he got the light gray tones, but I wasn't about to ask. Sometimes when Sensei wasn't around Tokida would lean over my shoulder and say, "Look at the statue. You see any black there?" I resented him, and wished I could work in a separate room. Once I sat behind him and watched him draw for a long time. He enjoyed that. The statue was pure white, and so was the paper, and Tokida was using solid black charcoal to bring the two together — drawing white on white. It didn't make much sense at first. The lightest shade Tokida made was far darker than the darkest shadow on the statue, and yet his drawing looked real and three-dimensional. I saw that he was creating an illusion. It was a big discovery for me.

❖   ❖   ❖

Mother came to Tokyo one weekend a month. She always came with gifts and Grandmother fussed over her like a housemaid — as if to make up for all the years she'd punished Mother with silence and neglect. There was always a lot to say after a month's separation, but our conversations were mostly gossip and small talk. I'd been waiting for an opportunity to tell Mother about Sensei, but Grandmother was always hovering in the background, not giving us a chance to be alone.

In the end I decided to visit Mother at her shop, which was in a fashionable shopping area in Yokohama. It was a small place with three glass counters and mirrored walls, with a storage room and a tiny windowless office in the back. Walking in there was like walking into a cloud of smells, fragrances of the things women use — face powder and perfume, cold cream and nail polish. The two girl clerks who worked for Mother gave me a friendly smile. One of them was pretty and it embarrassed me to look her in the eye. I didn't know why.

"Is she expecting you?" she asked me in a whisper. I shook my head. It gave me a strange feeling to realize that she was my mother's employee. Clumsily I waved to her not to bother and knocked on the office door.

"Come in," I heard Mother's voice say.

She was leaning over her neat desk, with an open ledger in front of her. An abacus lay across the ledger. As she looked up her face broke into a smile.

"Koichi, what a surprise," she said and leaned back on the

swivel chair, and nodded at the empty chair in front of her. I went and sat in the chair, feeling like someone on a job interview.

"What a nice surprise," she said again.

"I meant to write to you first. . . ." I started to apologize.

"Is there something the matter?"

"No, I thought I'd come and see you."

"How delightful. I like surprise visits. Have you had lunch?" I shook my head. "Let me finish this column and we'll go somewhere. Would you like a cup of coffee? Mari-san can run across the street and get you a cup."

"No, thank you." I shook my head. Mariko was the pretty clerk. We always drank tea at Grandmother's house, but Mother was fond of strong coffee.

She had on a finely knit lavender sweater with a brightly patterned silk scarf around her neck, held in place by a single pearl pin. Her lips glistened with deep rouge. Even her nails were painted. Grandmother didn't approve of cosmetics and in Tokyo mother dressed in somber colors and never wore makeup. On the wall behind her hung a framed picture of me taken a long time ago in Kyushu. Father had a copy of it in his album, but seeing it on Mother's wall always pleased me. Mother's fingers worked rapidly on the abacus, clicking the beads, and she entered the figures in the ledger with a dip pen. In about ten minutes she was finished.

"Let me treat you to your favorite dish." She looked up and smiled.

"Sweet and sour pork?"

"You were always such a fussy eater, but that's one dish you never refused. Is Grandmother well?"

"She's fine."

I noticed her tweed skirt when she went over to the corner to take some money out of the old safe. I'd never seen her in it before and thought it looked elegant on her.

Mother told Mariko we'd be out for about an hour and we walked out into the busy noontime street. I stood almost a full head taller than she, and I smelled her perfume as we walked along the covered sidewalk. Mother was a familiar figure in the neighborhood, and from time to time someone would stop and greet us with a bow. One time she told me that a store owner on the same block had seen us together and thought I was her brother, and she laughed about it. We went to a Chinese restaurant a couple of blocks down the street.

"Have you been eating regularly?" asked Mother as she took out a package of cigarettes from her purse. I nodded and struck a match to light it for her. That was another thing she didn't do in front of Grandmother — smoke. She gave the waitress our order — a dish of sweet and sour pork, fried wontons, and some Chinese greens — and turned to me.

"So, what is on your mind? I know you didn't come just to say hello."

"I wanted to talk to you before, Mother, but I didn't want to do it in front of Grandmother."

"I'm listening."

"Do you know who Noro Shinpei is?"

"What a funny name. I think I've heard it before."

"He's a cartoonist."

"Oh, yes, I remember. Didn't you have some of his books?"

"Yes, the same one. He's my teacher."

"What do you mean? Is he teaching at your school?"

"No, Mother, he's a famous cartoonist. I went to him and asked if I could be his pupil. He said yes."

"You went to see him, just like that?"

"Yes. You see, he took on an apprentice last year. I read about it in the paper and thought he might take me on, too. I didn't tell you anything before because I wasn't sure if he was going to say yes."

"So it's the tuition, is it?"

"No, Mother, there's no tuition. He gave me a test to see how well I draw and I passed it. That was all. He says if I mention anything about tuition he's going to throw me out. Do I have your permission to study with him?"

"Well, you've already committed yourself, haven't you? I know how important drawing is for you, Koichi, but so is your education. How are you going to manage your schoolwork?"

"I'll study hard, Mother, very hard, I promise. And if my grades go down I won't see Sensei till I'm doing better. I promise, Mother."

"Tell me more about your master."

I told her all I knew about Sensei. I also told her something about Tokida, leaving out his *yakuza* background. I talked about him as if he was a genius. But the thing that seemed to please her the most was that Sensei was a family man with a wife and two children.

"Does his wife use perfume?" asked Mother.

"I don't know, but it might be nice for a New Year's gift or something," I said, sensing things were going well for me.

"He must be an extraordinary person, taking on young men like you and your friend. He must think very highly of you. I'm glad."

"It's all right if I study with him then?"

"As long as you keep your promise, I don't see why not."

"You really don't mind if I become a cartoonist?"

"Koichi, when you were a small child, I used to worry about you constantly. You were always disappearing, running away from home when you could hardly walk, and we lived so near the beach. I used to worry about you drowning or falling down the staircase or being run over. Then the war came. And we survived it. After that I knew I could survive anything. The war has taught me something: Whatever is going to happen is going to happen. No, I don't worry anymore, Koichi. I'm only grateful that we're alive. And if you want to be an artist, then you must study art. You were drawing before you learned to walk, and it isn't for me to change that."

"What about Grandmother?" I said. "She won't think a cartoonist is respectable. I just know it."

"Grandmother comes from a proud family, Koichi. A little old-fashioned perhaps, but she means well. After all, you're her only grandchild. Don't be too hard on her."

"Will you talk to her?"

"Yes, I will, and I'll be tactful. Eat your lunch."

57

Mother showed more concern about my not eating than about my future, and I'd worried sick about breaking the news to her. What would Father have said in the same situation? I wondered. I was glad I didn't have to deal with him.

When we were finished with lunch, Mother paid the waitress and gave me some money. When Grandmother gave me my monthly allowance it was always businesslike, but with Mother I felt like a small boy again, receiving my pocket money and running out to buy whatever I wanted with it.

I didn't go back to the shop with Mother but said good-bye to her in front of a trolley stop. She said for me to thank Sensei for all he had done. She looked beautiful when Grandmother wasn't around. I wondered if she had a suitor. I couldn't imagine anybody who would be right for her.

NINE

❖ ❖ ❖ ❖ ❖

As it turned out, I'd gone to see Mother just in time. The following weekend, Mr. Kato came to the inn with a photographer. His editor-in-chief had decided to run a feature article on Sensei and wanted some photographs taken. Sensei was agreeable, and insisted that Tokida and I be included in the picture.

"Not me," said Tokida.

"Come now," coaxed Sensei, "think of your instant fame, the fan mail. Your friends back home."

"Should I shave then?" asked Tokida, rubbing his chin.

"Don't, Tokida," I warned him. "You'll cut yourself all over again."

Tokida was concerned with the way he looked, and that amused me. We weren't so different after all. I took out a comb and smoothed out my hair without looking in a mirror. When the photographer began to set up his equipment I felt nervous and had to go to the toilet. Sensei walked in and stood next to me. From the corner of my eye I saw a fresh-lit cigarette hanging from the side of his mouth. We looked at the back garden through the narrow slit of a window framing the lush, damp part of the garden like a horizontal scroll. The moss on the rocks looked especially green in the shadow of the inn.

"Kiyoi," said Sensei, looking straight ahead into the garden, "have you ever been in Korea?"

"No, sir."

"Land of the Morning Calm, they call it, a very beautiful country. A land of poets."

I said nothing.

"If you ever feel the need to talk to someone, don't hesitate to come over at any time. Some evening, when you have nothing else to do, come and stay with us."

"Thank you, sir," I said. Tokida must have told him about my father and also that I lived alone. I felt tears well up in my eyes. Sensei walked out before me, leaving a trail of smoke, without looking me in the eye, without saying another word.

The big-bellowed camera was set up on a tripod, and the photographer was fussing around the worktable, moving inkpots and brushes, taking out what he didn't like, and putting the latest issue of their magazine so the name of the publication showed clearly. Then he made us sit around the table, straightening Sensei's kimono collar. When he was pleased with the arrangement he put some powder on the flash plate and made nine exposures with blinding explosions.

"Why so many?" asked Tokida, blinking his weak eyes.

"This way we're certain to get at least one good shot," replied the photographer.

"I'd like some copies if you can spare them," said Sensei.

"Yes, of course, I'll have extra prints made for all of you. Now may I take a few more outside without the flash? Just Sensei this time."

"Why not?" Sensei complied, and the two of them went down to the garden.

"Are you really going to use our picture?" I asked Mr. Kato.

"Well, my assignment was to get some pictures of Sensei. But then my editor-in-chief hasn't met you young men. I have to admit it's a brilliant idea, including you two. A famous cartoonist and his two disciples. You don't hear stories like that anymore. I wish I'd thought of it myself. I think I'll tell the chief the inspiration was mine."

"I bet we'll be swamped with boys from all over the place, wanting to be cartoonists," sneered Tokida.

"Wait till your father sees your picture." I tried to humor him.

"That's right, gentlemen, you're going to be famous overnight, and you might as well get used to it. But more important, this article might cinch my promotion, and if it does I'll treat you to a movie, and that's a promise. On second thought, a restaurant, Sensei included," said Mr. Kato.

Tokida was his usual cool self and didn't seem in the least interested in seeing himself in a nationally circulated magazine. But I had a hard time hiding my excitement. Should I have smiled more? Should I have looked serious? Maybe I did smile, but couldn't remember.

I expected it to be at least a month before the article came out, but Mr. Kato was back in less than two weeks. He was in an unusually good mood as he took a stack of new magazines out of his briefcase. Fresh off the press, he announced proudly. Tokida and I didn't dare pick up the magazine, but anxiously watched Sensei as he flipped through the pages. And there we were, the three of us in a full-page photograph. Sensei looked more serious than usual, and Tokida looked into the camera with a twisted mouth that was between a smile and a sneer. But it was myself that I secretly pored over. I was nearest the camera and looked larger than the other two, and because of the lens distortion my hands and one foot that stuck out from under the table looked enormous. I wished I hadn't worn the silly grin on my face, but I did look friendly, and the picture pleased me. I looked at least as old as Tokida.

"A good shot, don't you think?" said Mr. Kato.

"Indeed," agreed Sensei. "A historical event. The likeness of Tokida is remarkable. What a trio of vagrants. I'll take five copies for posterity."

"And please take note of the great piece of writing that goes with it," said Mr. Kato. "I'll have you know I have been promoted; that's my literary debut, and I'm inviting you all to dinner as promised." He gave Tokida and me a broad grin.

A short article accompanied the photograph, mostly about Sensei, and a blurb about Tokida and me. Mr. Kato told us the magazine would be distributed throughout the country within a week.

That evening I went to see Grandmother. I knew Mother had told her about Sensei, but I hadn't seen her since then, so I had no idea how she was going to greet me. My visit surprised her, but before she could react I handed her the magazine. She put on her rimless glasses, held the magazine at arm's length, and when she recognized me in the photograph her mouth dropped open in surprise.

"Haa!" she exclaimed softly. She studied the cover, the back cover, inspected the spine of the thick magazine as if to see if it was real, then she went back to the photograph and stared at it.

"That's Sensei." I pointed to my master, realizing she was looking only at me.

"Not a handsome face, but it has dignity. He looks more like an author than a cartoonist," observed Grandmother. "And the one with pimples? Is he the boy from Osaka?"

"Yes, that's Tokida. He's three years older than I."

"A busy face, full of pressure, but intelligent. Some schooling would refine his face." She went back to looking at me. "Do you remember your grandfather?"

"A little. He was tall, wasn't he?"

"Very tall. You've taken after him. He was a handsome man when he was young."

She handed me the magazine. "Read the article for me," she said, closing her eyes to listen. I read her the blurb about Tokida and me, pronouncing my name the way Sensei did.

" 'In this special issue, we are pleased to introduce to our readers for the first time our best-known cartoonist, Noro Shinpei, and his talented assistants, Tokida Kenji and Kiyoi Koichi. Tokida, on the left, is a sixteen-year-old native of Osaka; he has been studying with Sensei for a year. Kiyoi, in the foreground, is a thirteen-year-old middle school student. He was born in Yokohama and attends the Aoyama Middle School here in Tokyo. Although the young men have been previously unknown to the public, our readers have been familiar with their work for some time, for it is Tokida and Kiyoi who put in the superbly drawn backgrounds for all of Noro Shinpei's serials. No doubt we will continue to enjoy their work in the years to come.' "

Grandmother sat still, with her eyes closed. For a moment I thought she had fallen asleep, but then I noticed she was working her lips. She seemed to be struggling not to smile.

"Koichi," she said and hesitated. "Where can I buy a copy of this?"

"I brought this for you."

"I will buy my own."

"Don't be silly, Grandmother. Sensei gave me an extra copy; this one is for you. And even if you wanted to buy one, it won't come out for another week."

"Thank you," she said.

The article caused quite a sensation at my school. Even the upperclassmen and teachers I had never had nodded to me in hallways. I was a celebrity!

"I always thought you were too good," said Abacus, the painting instructor. "Do you expect me to compete with your great master? Here, take this key to the art room and use it anytime you wish after school. As of now you're out of my hands; I refuse to have anything to do with your art education."

"But I don't know how to paint in oils," I protested.

"Nonsense. Noro Shinpei's disciple indeed!"

Abacus had always been kind to me. She gave me an A for everything I did, and she was the only teacher in school who was friendly to me.

But my new fame did nothing to improve my relationship with my classmates. I was never very popular with other students, and I didn't exactly go out of my way to make friends. So I thought it was strange when one of my classmates approached me the day the magazine came out. All I knew about him was that his parents were dead, and that he was the smartest boy in my grade.

"Hey, wait up, Sei," Mori called out. "Let me walk with you to the station. What made you decide to study cartooning?"

"I was bored with school."

"I don't blame you — school is a bore. I can't wait to be in college. But tell me about your master. Noro Shinpei, a strange pen name, isn't it?"

"He was a political cartoonist during the war," I told him. "Most people don't know that. He was against the war, and you know what that means. He had to go underground. I suppose that was when he adopted the name, to make fun of the military regime, and also to compensate for the fact he never served in the army."

"A brave thing to do, considering those who ruled us. Is he a Communist?"

"I never asked. I don't think so. I don't think a political cartoonist should have a leaning toward any given party. His job is to needle them equally, don't you think?"

"Everybody has to have a viewpoint, though. But I suppose you're right in a way. Is he funny?"

"He is, in a deep way."

"How many mistresses does he have?"

"I don't know."

"Come, Sei, you can tell me. All artists have mistresses. That's where they get their inspiration. Everyone knows that."

"Well, if he has a mistress I haven't met her. His wife is a good person."

"Everybody has a wife; it doesn't mean a thing. So what do you do when you go to your master's place?"

"Mostly I draw."

"No funny faces? Aren't you supposed to be learning to cartoon?"

"You can't go out and start drawing cartoons right away. You have to go through the same kind of training painters go through."

"Sounds like a hard discipline. How about nudes? Have you drawn nudes?"

"Yes. I go to Inokuma's studio twice a week."

"I've always wondered about those models. Are they shaved? I mean, pubic hair."

"Of course not."

"I envy you."

"Anyone can sign up to draw nudes."

"I don't mean that. I mean my future. It seems dull compared to yours."

"Why?"

"Studying economics. I want to make a lot of money. My parents didn't leave me very much. True, my rich uncle adopted me, but it's not the same as having my own money. What I really want to do is study history, but what can you do with a degree in history? I want to be a millionaire, and I intend to make it on my own," he said, and looked at me as if to find out what I thought. We were standing in the square in front of the station and I looked away, pretending to look for my bus.

"How about going to a movie some Saturday morning?" he said. "It's easy to get good seats then. Do you like coffee?"

"I do."

"Good. I know some good places. Bring your drawings, only the nudes. By the way, I know a girl who's interested in you. I'll tell you about her next time we meet," he said just before he got on the bus.

It was strange to hear him say that he wanted to be a millionaire; boys from good families weren't supposed to talk about money. There was something about him that made me feel uneasy. Perhaps it was his intense eyes that were too close together. He gave me the impression that he knew more about the world than the other students. But I decided to have coffee with him anyway — I wanted to find out who the girl was.

TEN
❖ ❖ ❖ ❖ ❖

The two evenings a week I spent in the life drawing class put a strain on my study time, so my visits to the inn were limited to weekends. I longed for the summer to come. I was full of good intentions: I would study hard to bring my grades up, write something in my diary every day, use up at least ten sketchbooks. But when the vacation began all my resolutions were quickly forgotten. I spent most of my days at the inn.

In the morning, when there was no work, Tokida and I would scan the paper to see what was happening in the city to plan our excursions.

Tokyo is a city of department stores, and that summer one of them installed an escalator, the first to be installed after the war. Tokida and I decided to go there on the grand opening day and try it out. But as it turned out we weren't the only ones. When we arrived, a huge mob was already massed around the entrance. A young woman, wearing what appeared to be a bus conductor's uniform, stood by the escalator greeting the riders, warning them to watch their step and to hold on to the railings.

"What a fool thing that is," said Tokida in amazement. "Look at her, Kiyoi, she has to stand there and bow to all these idiots who are too lazy to wait for the elevators."

"I don't see how she can stand it," I agreed. "Maybe it's only for today, though."

The escalator seemed like such a big waste to me. I could have run up the staircase faster than those moving steps.

"Let's go down and try it again," said Tokida when we got to the third floor.

"Are we the lazy idiots you spoke about?"

"Only one more time, but let's say hello to her this time."

We went down the staircase and once again waited behind the long line, and when our turn came we bowed to the woman and said hello. She bowed and greeted us mechanically, without even looking up.

"She's a bowing machine," I said.

"She didn't see us," said Tokida. "How would you like to do that all day long? I'd go mad in an hour. They can make a machine to do that, a robot with a loudspeaker sticking out of its mouth."

"But if you worked for someone you'd have to do what he told you," I said, remembering all the clerks who worked for my father.

"I say it's wrong to make people do something like that. I tell you, Kiyoi, I'm never going to work for anybody. I'll shine shoes first."

"I'm not either. I'll shine shoes with you."

We went up to the fourth floor and walked among counters that displayed all kinds of glassware and crystal. Women clerks were arranging and rearranging their wares, trying to look busy. Tokida went up to a large display stacked with fancy glasses on top of one another. There was a mirror behind it and the glass pyramid glittered under the strong light.

"What would you do if I ran my hand along the bottom and brought the whole thing down?" asked Tokida.

"I'd tell them I'd never laid eyes on you before."

"It's good to know you're a friend of mine. Wouldn't it be fun to break everything in a place like this? What do you think the clerks would do?"

"They'd send you back to Osaka, handcuffed this time."

"Don't you ever feel like going crazy sometimes, like smashing something just for the hell of it?"

"Sure, when I'm angry I feel like breaking things, and sometimes I do."

"I must be mad all the time then. It sure is fun to smash glasses. Just the sound of it makes me feel good. Crash!"

"Hey, let's get out of here before you go crazy. Let's go see the van Gogh show; it's around the corner from here."

"All right, let's. Maybe I'll slash some paintings."

The gallery was mobbed but we bought our tickets anyway. A narrow path had been roped off along the walls and we shuffled along with the crowd. We couldn't stop to study a painting, for the guards kept telling us to move on. It was a miserable way to look at the works of a master, but still the paintings fascinated me. I had seen a lot of reproductions on postcards, calendars, books, and such, but never an original. The difference was the comparison between seeing nude paintings and then seeing a live model for the first time. They were the clumsiest paintings I had ever seen, but there was something about all those violent swirls of paint that made my heart beat fast. I looked at Tokida. He was lost to the world. He had his head up against one of van Gogh's self-portraits — the one with a bandage wrapped around his head after he'd slashed his ear with a razor. Tokida was holding up the traffic but didn't seem to be aware of it. That was one thing I was beginning to find out about Tokida. When he got involved in something the world around him seemed to disappear. He had his glasses off and was scanning the painting, square inch by square inch, as though reading fine print.

"We'd better move on, Tokida; we're blocking the way," I whispered to him.

In the end I had to drag him outside. He would have lingered there till closing time.

"How do you expect to see anything with all those idiots climbing all over you?" he complained. "I'm coming back here tomorrow when they first open. I've never seen paintings like those."

"They're nothing like the reproductions, are they?"

"Did you see those eyes?"

"How could I? You were hogging the painting most of the time."

"You really don't have to have a great deal of technique, I guess."

"What do you mean?"

"I never painted portraits because I always thought eyes were too hard to paint. Eyelashes, eyelids, and all that. But he painted them like anything else. I mean he painted everything in the same way, do you know what I mean? He sort of drew them in with the brush, no smoothing out the edges, no fancy strokes. I want to start painting. We ought to talk to Sensei about it."

"I thought you weren't interested in becoming a painter."

"I'm not. But there's nothing wrong in painting a few pictures. I want to paint in oils for a while; it's so different from watercolor."

"I've never used oils either. They say it's easier than doing watercolors. If you make a mistake you can go right over it. Let's ask Sensei about it."

We walked along the main boulevard until we came to the Kabuki theater.

"Have you ever seen a Kabuki play?" asked Tokida.

"Once, the one about the famous *yakuza*. I couldn't understand a word of what they were saying. They speak in old Japanese."

"Sensei says even the old-timers can't make out what they say," he said and looked up at the tiers of tiled roofs on the tall theater. "Did you know that Delacroix said an artist has to be able to draw a man falling from the top of an opera house and finish it by the time the man hits the ground?"

"That's kind of hard on the model, isn't it?" I asked. Tokida burst out laughing.

"That's a good one, Kiyoi; we have to tell it to Sensei. Hard on

69

the model!" I didn't think it was that funny, but it was good to see him laugh.

After lunch we took a trolley and got off by the Imperial Palace and walked along the moat.

"Let's go to the park and draw trees or something," I said, and we headed toward the Hibiya Park.

The day was bright and hot, and it was pleasant to stroll by the deep moat and watch the water birds. The area was one of the few places in Tokyo where you had the feeling you were in a wide open space. It was lunchtime, and office workers in shirtsleeves were eating lunch on the grass.

Suddenly we heard sirens. First a policeman on a white motorcycle sped by, then two police cars, and two more after that, followed by a caravan of open trucks loaded with battle-ready policemen, wearing helmets and holding long wooden staffs straight up in the air like lances. In the distance we heard people shouting and singing. The noise was coming from the direction of the park entrance.

"It might be a riot," Tokida said. "Let's go and see."

"What do you want to see a riot for?"

"Who says it's a riot? It's probably a demonstration."

"What's the difference? They always turn into bloody riots."

"Don't be a coward. Don't you want to see some action? Have you ever seen a demonstration?"

"I've never been in one, if that's what you mean. And I don't intend to get mixed up in one."

"Don't be stupid; nothing is going to happen to us. And if you're afraid to come, I'll go by myself. I want to see what it's like."

"All right." I gave in. "But if you join them I'll leave."

"Of course I'm not going to join them. Let's go."

A huge crowd was gathering in front of the park entrance. They were mostly university students in white shirts and black trousers. There were also quite a few women milling around and I felt a little better. Many were waving placards and signs denouncing the government and the prime minister. Several men with rolled-up sleeves and headbands were directing the crowd, shouting through megaphones and telling the people the route they were to take, not to be afraid of the police, to keep calm, and so on. A convoy of trucks was parked nearby and the policemen were lining up along the boulevard like infantry soldiers before a big assault. They looked grim and ominous in their spotless black uniforms.

"It's a protest march," said Tokida.

"What are they protesting?" I asked.

"Who knows? I think they want to put the Socialist party in power. That's what they're always talking about anyway."

More and more demonstrators converged around the gate like bits of iron filings toward a magnet. Suddenly I realized that Tokida and I were inside the large circle of policemen. They kept their distance, but they had surrounded the demonstrators, and us. It probably wasn't too late for me to walk across the police line to the other side, but I was afraid to be confronted by those fearful policemen with their six-foot riot sticks. Tokida, also realizing that we were surrounded, grasped me by the arm and started to walk toward the crowd.

"What are you doing?" I cried in alarm. "I don't want to join these people," I said, and heard my voice crack.

"Look, nothing is going to happen to us, understand? It's just a protest march," he assured me.

Feeling angry and helpless, I looked over my shoulder and saw news photographers readying their big press cameras, safely behind the police line. My God, what if Grandmother sees my picture in the paper, I thought in a panic. What if Mother finds out I was demonstrating with university students? And what would they think of me at school? They wouldn't think. They'd throw me out before I could open my mouth. I felt a raging anger at Tokida. It was all his fault. Why had I listened to him?

But it was too late.

I was in it now, like a loach inside a bean cake. I had to get away from those photographers in a hurry. I had no choice but to join the crowd and get lost in it.

And how serious they looked! They were humming and singing

as if to work up courage. The smell of hair oil and perfume in the hot sun nauseated me, but I felt safe with all those bodies jostling around me. Tokida stood with his body pressed against my side, but I was too angry to talk to him. We stood in the tightly packed crowd for a good half hour, and I was beginning to worry about a place to urinate when the men with the megaphones shouted at us to move. The crowd stirred and surged forward. Three thousand? Five thousand? Maybe more, I had no idea. We took our first step awkwardly, like some gigantic centipede trying to coordinate its many legs. I was a dot in the sea of a faceless crowd. No camera would pick me out now. Why am I here? I kept asking myself. "Keep in line!" the leaders boomed at us. "Link up your arms! Don't break formation! Let's go!"

My sketchbook got in the way but somehow I managed to link arms with Tokida on my right and a university student to my left. For the first time I noticed Tokida was wearing his tennis shoes instead of the usual wooden clogs. Our linked arms were tense with excitement and I felt something like electricity run through my body. Soon we got into the rhythm of marching, the leaders keeping time with their silver whistles. The streets leading into the boulevard had been blocked off by the police, and we marched down the middle of the road and through the traffic lights. The white and yellow lines that divided the roads and the traffic signs that ordered the city life lost meaning. Common sense was forgotten; we were shouting in cadence in a thundering unison, like the men who carry the portable shrine during a summer festival. We zigzagged the width of the wide boulevard, weaving from sidewalk to sidewalk, unstoppable like the flow of lava, the marching army ants, mindless and devastating. There were faces sticking out of every window, and the sidewalks were lined with spectators. We were moving at half trot now, shouting at the top of our lungs, snaking like one enormous Chinese dragon, working up a frenzy. Nothing could stop us now. My pulse beat in time with the thousands of hearts all around me. There was a fever in my head, and I stopped thinking. I shouted till my lungs ached, though I didn't know why, and I could not hear my voice. I no longer had control over my own mind and body. Caught in the tremendous excitement and the power of the mob, I no longer knew who I was, and didn't care.

It seemed we marched for a long time, going around the city in a vast circle. We weaved between tall buildings, our shouting echoing like thunder. We poured out into a wide open space and the sky seemed suddenly to clear up. Straight ahead of us I saw the Diet building, the seat of Japanese government, looming above the sea of black heads and white headbands swaying and waving like the rolling of the sea. Policemen were stretched out in a long line in front of the building, their helmets shining in the sun, their staffs held like bayonets. We charged at them, almost running. I felt the terrible power of the stampeding mob.

But the police held their ground, barring our way with their sticks. The crowd spread out, cursing and yelling denouncements, thousands of bodies piling up from the rear.

"Bring out the prime minister!" I shouted with them. We pushed against the police and the police pushed back. Suddenly the immense mass of bodies staggered forward. The police line broke. Like water gushing out of a broken dam, the demonstrators burst through the gap and rushed toward the Diet building. Policemen were everywhere. Furiously they swung their sticks and the air was filled with the sound of heavy blows, screaming, and groaning. The man who had been linking arms with me stumbled forward as Tokida yanked away violently. My sketchbook fell to the ground and was instantly trampled. There was no more formation, no more order, no more cadence. People scattered and ran and tripped over one another. Some were throwing rocks and pebbles, anything they could get their hands on. Policemen jabbed and rammed their sticks. Blood flowed. I was crying from fear. Stricken with terror and confusion, I couldn't even move. From the corner of my eye I saw Tokida. His face was white. His cap was gone and he didn't have his glasses on. A thought flashed in my head: The fool can't see a thing without his glasses! Something glinted in his hand. The switchblade knife! Without thinking I leaped at him. "It's me, it's me! Drop that thing, you fool!" I screamed in his ear, grabbing his arm with both hands. I pulled him frantically, trying to change direction in the mad stampede. I knew instinctively that if we fell, we'd be trampled to death. I held on to Tokida with one hand and with the free arm swung at anybody who came our way. It was like fighting in a dream — there was no strength in my arm. But my grip on Tokida was like the grasp of an iron vise. Because of my height I could see where the police were; I shoved and elbowed and kicked our way, changing direction when I saw a helmet gleaming. The rioters were retreating now, dragging the wounded, women screaming, blood flowing bright on white shirts.

Abruptly the police stopped chasing the mob, as if on a cue, but kept their distance and began to regroup. The men with megaphones began to shout again, taunting the police and urging their comrades to get back into formation. I wouldn't have any of it. I kept running in the opposite direction, dragging blind Tokida by the arm.

"Let go! You're hurting my arm!" he shouted. "Let me put my glasses on, will you."

So he hadn't lost his glasses; he had taken them off when he saw the fight coming. But how could he see without them? I'd forgotten about the incident at the cutlery shop. Then I remembered Tokida's comment about slashing van Gogh's paintings. I should have known then he had a knife. As Tokida took out his glasses from his trouser pocket I saw blood on his hand.

"What's that from?" I pointed at his hand, feeling sick to my stomach.

"Thanks to you, I nearly lopped off another finger. When you grabbed me like an idiot and started to drag me, I tried to fold back the blade and the stupid thing cut me," he said, sucking on his index finger.

"Did you stab somebody?"

"Don't talk like a fool. Of course I didn't stab anybody."

"Why don't you try a sword next time, the kind you open up your belly with."

"Don't be an idiot. I was trying to protect you."

"Me! Protect me? Next time just worry about yourself. I never wanted to join those idiots. You could've killed somebody."

"What are you talking about? Do you know those brutes were ready to kill us? Stop talking so noble. Look at yourself; you've peed all over yourself."

I looked down at myself and sure enough I'd wet my pants and didn't even know it. But I was too angry to care.

"Who wanted to be in the demonstration in the first place? And what about that stupid knife of yours? You promised me you weren't going to buy it. You're a liar!"

"I promised you nothing. And if it wasn't for you grabbing me, I'd still have the knife."

"Why did you join them? What the hell were they demonstrating about anyway? Tell me that!"

"Wait a minute, Kiyoi, wait just one minute. I don't have to stand here and listen to a thirteen-year-old lecture me."

"I'm going to be fourteen in a few days."

"I beg your pardon," he sneered. "So tell me, old man, what's wrong with demonstrations? Or strikes? What's wrong with people wanting better jobs, more money, or a better government? Maybe you were raised with everything you ever wanted, but most people aren't that lucky. What's wrong with people trying to change this stupid world? Remember that woman at the department store? How would you like to do that for ten hours every day? You wouldn't last a day. Did you ask for the war? Did you ask your ma and pa to get a divorce? You think I asked to be born into this world, with a father as vicious as one of those brutes out there? Do you think my old man and ma thought about me when they first had sex? I don't give a damn about any of them; I hate them all! Sensei's the only good man I know."

"But you almost had us killed," I said, losing steam. "Look, they're still going at it." I nodded toward the Diet building.

"It's no good talking like this," said Tokida. "Let's get out of here. Here, take this and cover yourself." He handed me his raggedy jacket. "And don't tell Sensei any of this."

"I won't tell if you throw your knife in the river."

"I told you, I don't have it. Two thousand seven hundred yen down the drain. You're pretty strong for your age," he said and rubbed his arm where I'd grabbed him.

I didn't believe he'd lost his knife, but said nothing.

ELEVEN

❖ ❖ ❖ ❖ ❖

It was still early when I got home that night. I took a change of clothes and went to a bathhouse. When I returned it was getting dark and I saw a light in my next-door neighbor's window. I knocked on the door.

"Come in," said Mr. Kubota. The door was unlocked so I went in, thinking that a karate expert never has to lock his door.

"Sei-san! Come in and have a seat; this'll take only a minute," he said, rinsing a pair of socks and a shirt in the washbasin.

"Am I interrupting you?" I asked out of politeness.

"Not at all. You came at the right time. Got a loan from my rich aunt and finally paid off my wine man, so my credit's good again. Got some beer and a bottle of the red stuff over there. Go in and open a beer; it's still nice and cold."

Two sweating bottles of beer and a full bottle of port wine stood on his desk. A book lay open under the desk lamp with pencil scribblings on the margins, and three pencils with the lead sharpened as thin as needles lay together like some surgical instruments on a doctor's table. There was something maddening about his orderliness. It was the sort of neatness Tokida would like to disrupt. I poured some beer into a teacup and took a sip. I was beginning to like its bitter taste.

"You can't wear the same shirt twice in this humid weather. I say it's time to shop for a wife," said Mr. Kubota, hanging the shirt and socks from a cord stretching across the open window. He put on his summer kimono and sat down.

"You haven't been around much lately," he said. "Some *gahru frendo?*"

"No, nothing like that," I said. I wondered why grown men liked to tease you about girl friends. "I've been working with Sensei."

"How does it feel to have your future secure at your age? What do you plan to do with your spare time?"

"I was wondering if you'd be willing to teach me karate."

"Why karate? I'd think with your background you'd lean toward swordplay," he said and sipped out of the beer bottle. He stared me in the eye even as he lifted the bottle to his lips, and it made me nervous. His were the eyes of a martial-arts expert, steady and calm eyes that never missed a thing.

"But isn't it true that karate is the most useful thing to know when you have to go against a crowd, like in a street fight, for instance?"

"Were you in a street fight?"

"No, nothing like that, Mr. Kubota. I accidentally got mixed up in a demonstration."

"The one in front of the Diet building? I heard about it; many of my friends were there. Some of them were hurt rather badly. A bad business, Sei-san; you must stay away from that sort of thing."

"I know, it was terrible; it was like war. But it was an accident, really. Did you ever get mixed up in something like that?"

"I avoid violence on principle. Tell me about the riot."

"We didn't throw rocks at them or anything, but they came after us anyway. They were ready to club us to death."

"Who is us?"

78

"Tokida and I."

I had meant to leave Tokida out of it, not wanting to mention his knife, but I had made a slip and there was no turning back now.

"He's Sensei's other pupil," I said. "He's seventeen. Anyway, he lost his glasses in the fight, and he can't see a thing without them, so I had to drag him all over the place, trying to get away; we were lucky we didn't get trampled to death."

"Is that why you want to learn karate? To fight the police?" He stared at me, narrowing his eyes.

"No, Mr. Kubota, I only want to be able to defend myself. Those people were wild; we had to fight our way out. It wasn't just the police — everybody was attacking us. I don't want to hurt anybody, Mr. Kubota; I only want to learn to defend myself the next time."

"The best thing is to make sure there won't *be* a next time. I tell you right now, Sei-san, the first law of karate is to run. When you see a fight coming, run the other way. I know very well what you're saying, but your basic premise is wrong. I'm willing to train you only if you regard it as a sport, and nothing else. Something to shape your body and perhaps improve your character. After all, that's what the martial arts are about."

"I probably won't be good at it anyway." I looked away.

I discovered that if I take a negative attitude about things — as long as I don't overdo it — people will encourage me. Mr. Kubota was no exception.

"Come now, that's no way to talk," he said. "Maybe karate will give you more self-confidence, and a little discipline may be a good thing."

"You'll teach me, then?"

"Why not? Come to the gym tomorrow and we'll start you out. Anytime after lunch."

"Thank you, Mr. Kubota; it means a great deal to me. I'll see you tomorrow." I bowed to him and left.

Once in my room I stared in the mirror above the washbasin and tried to look ferocious. I bared my arms and flexed my biceps. I had puny arms. I swished my right hand in the air and imagined it sinking into a policeman's helmet, then another slash, breaking a riot stick in half as though it were a chopstick. I'd been the worst athlete in all the seven schools I'd been to, and my classmates used to groan when they had to have me on their team. I kept looking in the mirror, twisting my mouth and rolling my eyes like an angry samurai. If I worked hard, perhaps I'd be as good as Mr. Kubota. Anyone with a second-degree black belt *had* to be deadly.

Next day I went to the university gym right after lunch. Mr. Kubota was instructing seven men lined up in a single row on the hardwood floor. They were all barefooted, wearing the white karate *gi*, the two-piece suits similar to those the judoists wear. Mr. Kubota was the only black belt there; the others had on the plain white belts.

"One!" shouted Mr. Kubota, and the men took a long step forward, striking out with their right hands at the same time, and froze in place. "Hold your fist straight!" he barked at one of the men. "Mikami, straighten your leg behind you! Two!" he shouted again, and as the men took their step and thrust their left arms, Mr. Kubota grasped one man's wrist and yanked him forward. The man lost his balance and stumbled. "Don't reach out with your body! A judo man would've thrown you clear across the room!"

Mr. Kubota wasn't the friendly neighbor anymore, but a stern and fearsome master of discipline. One, two! One, two! He barked the cadence like a drill sergeant and seemed to glide among the men like a panther. He never missed a thing. The harshness of the training surprised me, but then I'd never seen martial-arts training before. I remembered reading about a sword master who put out his own son's eye during a mock duel to show him the seriousness of sword fighting. I began to wonder if I was ready for this sort of thing. But I'd asked Mr. Kubota to teach me and wasn't about to lose face in front of these men. After about half an hour Mr. Kubota gave a signal for the men to take a break.

"Well, what do you think?" he asked, wiping the sweat off his face with a towel.

"I'd like to learn," I said. "I like it because you don't have to fight on the floor like in judo."

"It isn't anything like judo. Come, I have a spare suit you can use for today," he said and took me to the locker room. I put on the uniform and wore a white belt with his name stitched on it. It was reassuring to know that Mr. Kubota was a beginner once.

He worked with me for a few minutes, showing me how to stand, to make a fist, and to hit with the first two knuckles of my hands without moving my shoulders. They were some basic movements, he said, but anything that required physical coordination was difficult for me. I had always thought of karate as a mysterious, secret ritual, but now I realized it was mostly hard work.

After a while Mr. Kubota made me stand in front of a full-length mirror and practice by myself. The person I saw in the mirror didn't seem like someone who could break one single roofing tile with his bare hands, to say nothing of a six-foot riot staff, or a steel helmet. The other men ignored me out of politeness and I went on with my exercise. I didn't want to let Mr. Kubota down.

My body felt numb when I left the gym after an hour. Walking along the campus building, I tapped my knuckles against the wooden sidings, hoping they'd grow hard and lethal overnight. I felt healthy and hungry.

Outside the university gate was a large bookstore, and looking in the window I thought about Tokida and the van Gogh exhibit. A book of van Gogh's letters had been published recently, and I thought how good it would be to get it for Tokida. He would really like that. I went into the store.

"Do you have the book of van Gogh's letters?" I asked.

"*Dear Theo*," the clerk said, without looking up. "Look under biography. If it isn't there check under art. And if you don't see it there, it's a special order."

In the art section I got sidetracked by thick art books with color plates in them, forgetting all about van Gogh's letters. As I thumbed through an expensive new book I hadn't seen before, I saw a painting that took my breath away. It was a small portrait of a young woman. Her hair was done up in a big bun at the back of her head, and she wore a plain black velvet dress with a plain round collar. Her face was turned three quarters to the right, looking straight ahead. Her nose was too big; her lower lip

81

was thick and broad, and her heavy eyelids made her eyes seem dreamy, drowsy even. It was the most beautiful face I had ever seen, but like a vandal, Degas had scribbled his name right above her head. I stared at her eyes with great concentration, hoping somehow she'd turn her eyes to look at me. It was that kind of painting.

I was standing in a busy narrow lane and people brushed against me trying to reach around me for books. I had an uncomfortable feeling that everyone in the store was watching me. So every time I felt someone near me, I unconsciously held the book close to my body to hide the painting. I memorized the page number, put the book back on the shelf, and walked out.

It wasn't until I got on a crowded train that it occurred to me that I could have bought the book. But I was glad I hadn't. I'd also forgotten to get the van Gogh book and felt bad about that. I had wanted to surprise Tokida with it.

I stood in the packed aisle of the train and stared absentmindedly at a young woman by the automatic door. She stood with her back to me, listening to a man in a university uniform. As her head bobbled busily above her pink kimono collar while she nodded to everything the man was saying, something clicked in my mind. Her hair was tied in a bun like Degas's girl. I wiggled through the crowd to get near the couple, hoping she'd turn her head. I had to see her face. But the most I saw of her face was a three-quarter view, from the back. The soft round curve of her cheek thrilled me.

Two stations later, when the door opened, the couple stepped out. A kind of panic seized me, and without thinking I rushed out after them. I walked quickly, almost at a trot, and took in a whiff of camellia oil on her hair as I passed them. When I reached the staircase I turned around abruptly as if I'd forgotten something, and got a good look at her. She was still listening to the man, completely unaware of me or anything else in the world. She had a round face and chubby nose, and when she laughed a gold-capped tooth glinted inside her mouth. I wished I had not seen her face.

After that I went to the gym three days in a row, not so much to take my karate lessons, but to look at Degas's painting afterward. It was amazing how a painting could look so different from day to day. One day she'd seem pensive, on another day happy, and sometimes indifferent. And each time I saw her I tried to capture her image in my mind and draw her later from memory.

TWELVE

❖ ❖ ❖ ❖ ❖

"You haven't been ill, have you?" asked Sensei, lying on the floor with a book in his hand.

Tokida, who was drawing Venus de Milo, looked up and told me with his eyes not to mention anything about the demonstration.

"I had to run some errands for Grandmother," I lied. I hadn't been to the inn since the day of the riot, and felt a little guilty about it.

"Do you think we're ready to paint in oil?" I asked Sensei.

"So you've come down with van Gogh fever, too. Tokida's been pestering me for three days. Maybe I ought to see the exhibit myself."

"You really should, Sensei," said Tokida. "You really can't tell what the paintings are like by looking at reproductions. They have one of his palettes in a glass case. It's got paint all over it, so you can really see how he worked. I like it better than some of his paintings. You could tell he was mad."

"His violence appeals to you," said Sensei. "You must like

Sesshu's late works then, the same kind of masculine staccato strokes. I know what you mean about the palette. I like to look at unfinished works of masters; they tell you more about the artists than the finished works. There's something human about them."

"Do you like Degas?" I asked.

"I had my Degas period. You're in good company, Kiyoi. Toulouse-Lautrec, Picasso, and me. Degas was strongly influenced by the invention of the camera. Next time look at the way he composed his canvases. You'll notice a lot of things going off the edges, like in a bad snapshot — something we cartoonists have since perfected."

"I like his pastels and drawings better than his oils," said Tokida.

I knew nothing about Degas's composition, though I understood that he was a great draftsman. As far as Tokida was concerned, van Gogh was *the* painter. Neither Sensei nor Tokida mentioned Degas's girl. I would keep her to myself.

It was dark when we left the inn. It had stopped raining and the lights of the city reflected off the wet pavement. Sensei walked briskly as if he had a destination in mind. Maybe he's taking us to a cafe, I thought, even a bar. But it was an artists' supply shop he took us to, the largest I'd ever seen. There were more things there than I ever thought artists would need or use. Frames and statues and cheap prints hung on the walls. There were little collapsible easels, and the big studio easels that rolled on wheels, canvases that came in rolls and those that were already stretched, shelves and shelves of watercolors and oil paints, gouaches, papers, on and on and on.

"This has to be the most wonderful place in Tokyo," said Sensei, bending down and looking into the glass display case. "Every time I come here I feel like a boy in a toy store."

He was looking at the expensive English watercolors and French oil paints.

"Isn't it Noro Shinpei?" asked the clerk behind the counter.

"I'm afraid it is. I can't seem to stay away from your marvelous store."

"It's a pleasure to have you, sir. We received a large shipment of bristol boards since I saw you."

"I'm well supplied with those, thank you."

"Is there something special you're looking for then?"

"These oils here — I'd like two of everything."

Tokida nudged me with his elbow.

"Two of everything, sir?"

"Yes, meet Tokida and Kiyoi, so-called disciples of mine, two aspiring painters."

"This is indeed an honor." The clerk smiled at us. Tokida and I bowed to him.

"Have you been painting long?"

"They're only starting," answered Sensei. "What's a good brand these days?"

"Of course the French make the best, but if the young gentlemen haven't worked much in oils I should think the domestic paints would be quite adequate, and not so expensive."

"Then the domestic brand it is. Let me have two of these boxes, but if you don't mind I'd like to choose the colors myself. I also don't like the look of these brushes in the kit."

"No problem, sir. This kit is for display purposes, though a lot of beginners prefer it with our special discount. But then you're entitled to our twenty percent professional discount, sir. I'll get the boxes from the back room while you make your selections."

Tokida and I were speechless. We stared at the two walnut boxes the clerk brought out of the back room. Each had a metal lining inside, with compartments for brushes and paints and oil pots. Inside the cover was a folding palette with a thumb hole. Sensei called out the names of colors he wanted in the boxes, all English names that sounded strange and delicious — lemon yellow, carmine, rose madder. They sounded like the names of something cool to eat, like jellied fruit.

When everything was packed Sensei sent us out of the store with our packages. From the doorway we saw him produce a big wad of money from his kimono sleeve.

"How much do you think all this came to?" asked Tokida.

"I don't know, but a lot. He doesn't want us to know," I said.

"Well," said Sensei, joining us. "The rest is up to you."

"Thank you, sir." Tokida and I started to bow.

"No ceremonies. A token of my appreciation for all your hard work. Come, a celebration is in order. We're a few days early, I think, but let's celebrate Kiyoi's birthday," said Sensei and took us to a cafe.

It was obvious that Tokida talked a good deal to Sensei when I wasn't around, for I hadn't mentioned anything about my birthday to Sensei. I felt a little jealous of their closeness, but then it was mostly through Tokida that the master knew certain things about me — the things I would hesitate to tell him myself.

Tokida and I wasted no time. The very next weekend we took a train south, to a place from where we could see Mount Fuji. We walked on the country roads with our paint boxes slung from our shoulders and looked at farmhouses. Tokida was not impressed with the scenery; everything looked too ordinary, he complained. And I wasn't interested in painting the great mountain. We were looking for some exotic scene, some place that looked like the south of France van Gogh had painted, with windmills, red tiled roofs, and cypress trees that looked like flames. But in the end we set up our traveling easels and painted the drab farmhouses.

"This is harder than I thought," I said to Tokida. He came over and looked at the mess I was making, but for once he couldn't give me advice. We sat on the grass and laughed. He was happy in the sun, talking about van Gogh. I thought how good it would be to have a studio of my own one day, with a tall ceiling and big window that faced the north. Portraits are the hardest things to paint, and that was what I wanted to paint most of all.

❖   ❖   ❖

At the end of August I turned fourteen and Mother gave me a camera. I'd been wanting a camera for a long time and the gift delighted me. It was a small camera with a black leather bellows, a small prism for a viewer, but no range finder. Hoping I was focusing on the right place, I had to guess the distance between me and the subject to set the camera.

School began a few days after my birthday. I took up Abacus's offer and started to use the art room after classes. It was large and quiet, and I felt comfortable there. Many easels stood stacked in one corner, and along the tall wall were the statues of the discus thrower, Michelangelo's *David, Brutus, Venus de Milo,* whose nipples someone had blackened, and a couple of others I didn't know. It was the nearest thing to having my own studio. Though Venus was familiar to me, David was the first piece I tackled. I wanted to draw a male face for a change. His curly hair was hard to draw, and I was determined to learn to draw faces.

One day as I was drawing David with great concentration, a strange thing happened to me. I heard a kind of buzz inside my head, as if something had plugged up my ears, and I felt suddenly cut off from everything around me. My body went numb. I watched my hand holding a long stick of charcoal, moving up and down against the paper like the hand of a marionette. Then I felt myself wafting upward, leaving my body on the stool. Up and up I went, floating up to the ceiling. I was now a big eyeball, hovering against the ceiling, looking down at the room below me. I felt nothing, and saw everything — the cracks on the walls, paint smudges on the easels, the wide gaps between the wooden slats where the nails had come off. But strangest of all, I was watching myself, drawing like a mechanical man, with my right hand working on the paper.

I didn't know how long I had been up there when the sharp shrill of a whistle startled me. As in a dream I floated, falling and falling, back into my body. Suddenly I felt the weight of my raised arm. Like a sleepwalker I shuffled to the window and looked out to the playfield. Boys in striped shirts were playing soccer and the gym teacher was running with them, blowing his whistle. Had I been dreaming? Was I going mad? But there, leaning against the easel, was the drawing. It wasn't finished, but the rough shading and the outline looked like they'd been drawn by an expert. A shudder went through my body. It was the best drawing I had ever done and I had no idea how I had done it.

After that I locked myself in the art room every afternoon to see if it would happen again. It didn't happen often, but when it did, my drawings seemed too good to be my own work. It was as if I'd discovered something in me that I didn't know was there. Power to work magic. Did all artists experience such a thing? I wondered. If so, why hadn't I heard about it? Maybe it was too insane to tell anybody. Maybe it was the secret of art. I felt a great elation. Whatever it was, I would keep it to myself.

Also I was beginning to manage my time better and to concentrate on my studies more. But my social life at school, except for my casual friendship with Mori, didn't improve much. Mori and I occasionally had coffee together, and he taught me what he said was the proper way to drink it. He said a good cup of coffee had to be strong and rich enough to hold cream on the surface without mixing, and the coffee was supposed to be drunk through the layer of cream. According to him there were only three places in Tokyo where they served such coffee. He took me to all three, and teased me about some girl who was supposed to have a crush on me. But whenever I asked Mori who it was he would mention a different girl, so after a while I stopped asking him. We talked mostly about books, especially love stories, like *Lady Chatterley's Lover*. Mori paid a small fortune for a copy of that book, for it was banned in Japan, and lent it to me. I read one passage over and over until I could recite it backward. I kept the book three weeks.

THIRTEEN
❖ ❖ ❖ ❖ ❖

At the end of October all the students in the second year went on a day's outing to the seashore of Chiba, a prefecture north of Tokyo. There were three classes in my grade, with about fifty students each, and it was only on those excursions that the students from the classes mingled with one another.

I took a whole roll of pictures that day, guessing distances and lens openings, hoping for the best. The girls posed for me willingly, and even many of the teachers asked me to take their pictures. But Mori was the most eager subject of all, though when I first showed him my camera he said it was a primitive piece of machinery.

I was happy and excited when all the pictures turned out well, and I pored over them with satisfaction. Mori was in many of the shots, always clowning with his big eyes. One picture in particular came out clearer than the rest — a photograph of three girls from Mori's class on the beach with the white sky in the background. The chubby girl on the right was grinning, holding a dead crab, and the girl on the left had her eyes closed. I stared at the tall girl in the middle; her name was Okamoto Reiko, and she seemed to look back at me with a faint smile. I'd seen her many times before, but never paid much attention to her. Now I looked at her carefully; her hair came down to her shoulders, and the wind had caught it, revealing the oval shape of her face. There was stillness in her eyes, and her broad lower lip curved out. In my mind I rearranged her hair and gave her a big bun at the back of her head, then put a black velvet dress on her, with a plain round collar. My heart began to beat fast. The Degas painting! I had to see Reiko.

But it was Friday afternoon. Two whole days before I would see her in school. Then I remembered the little book the school had issued us when I was first admitted. The book had all the addresses and telephone numbers of students and teachers. A private telephone was expensive, but most of the students came from wealthy families. I was in luck — she had a telephone. I ran out of the house and rushed to the nearest public phone booth.

I wasn't used to calling people on the phone. I'd used it no more than a dozen times and felt like an idiot every time I had to talk into the machine. What should I say to her? Calling up a girl was almost unheard of. Maybe her mother or a housemaid would answer and report me to the principal; I was shaking from nervousness as I put a coin in the slot and dialed the number.

"Okamoto residence," said a woman's voice.

"Hello, may I trouble you to let me speak with Reiko-san?" I said in my best voice.

"May I tell her who's calling, please?"

"Kiyoi, no, I mean Sei. My name is Sei."

A pause.

"One moment, please," said the voice.

Sounds too formal, must be the maid, I told myself. She's taking an awfully long time coming to the phone . . . probably lives in a mansion . . . Looking out the glass panel I saw yet another man join the waiting line.

"Hello?" said a female voice.

"Okamoto-san?" I asked. She had a deeper voice than I expected, and I had a hard time putting her face to the voice.

"Yes?"

"This is Sei. I'm in Mr. Sato's class, you know, Goldfish."

"Yes?" she said again. She sounded as if she didn't know what I was talking about.

"Do you remember the picture I took of you on the beach the other day? Well, I got it back today and I'd like to give it to you."

"That's very nice of you. I'm sure the other girls would like to see it, too."

"I thought you might like to have yours first. It's really a good picture of you."

"Couldn't you give it to me at school?"

"Yes, but I didn't want to do it in front of other students."

"Couldn't you send it to me then?"

"I could, but I wanted to give it to you in person."

"How do you mean?"

"I thought perhaps you could meet me somewhere."

"Oh . . . Mother wouldn't approve. . . ."

"No, I suppose not. But couldn't you see me anyway? Without telling your mother?"

"I don't know . . . Where?"

"You live in Setagaya, don't you? I can come to the station."

"Someone might see us."

"What about Shibuya then? In front of the dog statue."

"I don't know."

"I only want to give you the picture. I thought maybe we could have coffee somewhere."

"Oh, Mother wouldn't approve of that sort of thing."

"No coffee then. Can you see me just for a few minutes?"

"When?"

"Tomorrow morning?"

"I have a piano lesson."

"In the afternoon then?"

"I'll have to think about it."

"Look, I'll tell you what. I'll be at the dog statue at three to-morrow afternoon."

"I'll have to think about it."

"Three o'clock. I have to hang up now. I hope you'll come. Good-bye."

There were now six people lined up outside the booth and they greeted me with stony silence. Did they hear me trying to arrange a date with a girl? Well, I would never see them again.

I walked slowly back to my room, trying to remember what her voice sounded like. It would be thrilling to hold hands with her, even for a brief moment. Small children do it all the time. So do adults. But we weren't children anymore, and not yet fully grown. For us holding hands or meeting on our own simply wasn't done. But were all girls as dense as Reiko? Why couldn't she make up her own mind? Her mother wouldn't approve! Piano lessons! She was probably taking tea lessons and flower arranging, also. It was all too bad. She was the only girl I knew who looked like Degas's painting.

❖ ❖ ❖

I arrived at the Shibuya station at two, full of hope and anxiety. I positioned myself next to a telephone pole across the square so I could keep a sharp lookout on the dog statue. And leaning against the pole I pretended to read a newspaper while rehearsing all sorts of lines in my head. Should I give her the picture right away, or wait till we got to an art gallery, or even a cafe? But then I didn't want to alarm her. I wouldn't think of doing something her mother wouldn't approve. A stroll through Meiji Park? A museum in Ueno? A movie would take too much time. If I could only see her for a moment perhaps I could talk her into meeting me again.

As three o'clock approached I got all the lines mixed up and didn't know what I was thinking anymore. Maybe she's standing somewhere and spying on the dog statue, too, I thought suddenly. So I crossed the square and walked to the statue, fumbling with my newspaper. One by one smiling faces appeared out of nowhere, paired up with somebody who'd been standing near me, and disappeared into the crowd, happy as imbeciles.

At three-thirty an old man with a beat-up felt hat and a box camera coaxed his toothless wife to pose in front of the statue and snapped a picture of her. Then they changed places, the old man telling his wife that all she had to do was to push on the shutter. She couldn't find it. I thought of taking the picture for them but felt too depressed even to offer.

She never came.

FOURTEEN

❖ ❖ ❖ ❖ ❖

Going to school was dreadful after that. Reiko was cool and indifferent, and acted as though we had never had our conversation. She seemed vacant, as if she had no feelings. Maybe she wasn't too bright, but that thought didn't cheer me up. I never gave her the picture.

Mori was full of praise for my snapshots, and was delighted when I gave him all the ones that included him. I showed him all the pictures, hoping he'd notice the one of Reiko and tell her something about it.

"You have the eye of an artist, no doubt about it," he declared. "And that lens of yours is sharp as anything Zeiss makes." He picked up the one of the three girls and studied it with a knowing smile.

"You're a sly one, Sei. How did you guess?"

"Guess what?" I asked.

"Don't play innocent with me. You know what I'm talking about."

"No, I don't."

"You know one of them has a crush on you."

"We're not going to go through that again, are we? You mention a girl every time I see you, and it's a different name each time," I said sarcastically, hoping he wouldn't notice me flushing.

"Don't pretend with me, Sei; I've told you about her before. It's the same one. You have a short memory when it comes to names."

"If you mean the one with the dead crab, I think she's rather pretty, too," I said. Mori fell for it.

"Don't be a fool. And I don't mean the moron standing next to her either."

"Let me guess. The one whose eyes are forever closed to me?"

"What do you expect? You made her nervous."

"Here, give her the picture, with my compliments."

"Any message?"

"No."

"You have nothing to say to her?"

"Why should I? I'm not interested in her."

"Say hello to her or something, at least."

"Look, if you like her so much, buy her a cup of coffee at one of your special places."

"To hell with you, Sei," he said and walked off.

One day during the morning assembly in the auditorium, a girl sitting next to me slipped a paperback book onto my lap. Slowly I turned my head around to make sure no one was watching and put the book in my coat pocket. I looked at her from the corner of my eye and whispered, "Thank you." My face flushed. She didn't look at me, but pretended to listen to the featured speaker on the stage.

Her name was Nakano Michiko. She was not in my class, but she'd been assigned the seat next to me since the new term began. I'd spoken to her a few times before, making snide comments about boring lectures, and she had nodded and smiled politely. I now studied her with quick sidelong glances. Her hair was cut straight across her forehead, and also on the back of her neck. She was one of the few girls who wore a school uniform, a pleated skirt of navy blue and a shirt with a sailor suit collar. The drab clothes and her schoolgirl haircut made her look plain, but now I saw that she was rather pretty.

The book was a work by Soseki, the great Japanese writer. Opening it in the art room that afternoon I found a note inside.

If you have not read this, please keep it. You'll think me stupid, but the man in the story reminded me of you.

Nakano

I read the thin handwriting over and over again. It was the first note I had ever received from a girl and it excited me tremendously. I was flattered, and had enough sense to know Michiko was telling me that she liked me. I read the book eagerly to find out what I had in common with the man in the book.

It was a strange tale of a man in his thirties, a painter who would scribble a poem every time something interested him. And the plot of the book was about his long vacation in a mountain inn and his encounter with a young woman who could read his mind. The book gave me an eerie feeling. If Michiko saw a similarity between me and the hero, she understood literature far more than I did.

"Thank you for the book," I whispered to her next day at assembly.

"Did you read it?" she asked without turning her head.

"I read it last night."

"Isn't it a wonderful book?"

"I liked it very much."

"I don't understand how he knows so much about women," she whispered.

"You think the woman is real?" I asked in surprise.

"Oh, yes. I often feel the way she does."

I thought about that for a while. Most likely it was the woman in the story who reminded Michiko of *herself*. The hero was probably an excuse to let me know how she felt about me.

"Did you read about the man who killed himself in Nikko?" asked Michiko.

I nodded. In the morning paper was an article about a man who had jumped from the top of the waterfall at Nikko, a well-known summer resort in the north. It was a popular place for committing suicide. The news was that they hadn't found the man's body.

"He's causing a lot of trouble," I said. "Why couldn't he have done it in a place where they wouldn't bother to look for his body? Jumping into a volcano would've been better."

Michiko gave me a quick look. "But don't you think it's egoistic to kill oneself?"

I nodded knowingly. I didn't know what she was talking about.

A few days later I gave her a book during meditation. It had been translated from German, but I felt a closeness to its hero, who lived alone in a boarding house. It didn't matter if she'd read it before, I wanted her to have my copy. We were now even in terms of gifts.

That afternoon I ran into Michiko in a bookstore near the Shibuya station. Actually I wasn't aware of her until she called my name. I blushed and started to stammer. I had the feeling our meeting wasn't an accident.

"Thank you for the book," she said and bowed to me in the narrow lane. "I'm glad you like Hesse. Have you read *Demian*?"

I shook my head.

"It's a lovely book. It's the kind of book you like to keep to yourself and not tell anyone about. Are you angry with me?"

"Why should I be angry?" I looked at her.

"For meeting you here."

"No, why should I? Are you looking for something special?"

"I'm just looking," she said and scanned the shelf in front of us. "Do you ever visit your friends?"

"I don't have many friends," I replied.

"I don't either. I like to be alone and read books. I spend all my allowance on books."

"I like to read, too, but I spend most of my free time at Sensei's studio."

"Your cartoon master? He must be a wonderful person. His serials are so amusing."

Michiko didn't seem like someone who read comic strips, and I wondered if she read Sensei's serials because of me.

"Sei-san," she said and hesitated. "Will you be angry if I ask you to come to my house some weekend?"

"No," I said and looked away. I had never expected an invitation from a girl. And Michiko's invitation meant that she'd already asked her parents' permission to bring me home. Whatever she'd told her parents about me must have been good.

"I don't mean for you to decide now, but my family, especially my father, would like very much to meet you."

"I'd like that," I said. "It would be an honor to meet your family."

"Will this Saturday be too soon?"

"No, I have nothing planned."

"It's best if I meet you somewhere. You'll never be able to find our house."

"I can meet you in front of the dog statue," I said without thinking.

"Would two o'clock be all right?"

"Yes, that's fine."

"I'm glad you can come." She bowed and left me standing in the narrow lane. I had my first date in front of the dog statue after all.

She was there before me, and I almost didn't recognize her in a smart blazer and a wool skirt. It was wonderful to see her waiting for me. As I crossed the square and walked toward her, she spotted me and smiled nervously. She was very pretty.

"Have you been waiting long?" I asked, even though I knew I was on time. She shook her head and looked away.

"Do we have to go to your house right away?" I asked.

"No, but I'd like you to have supper with us."

"With your family? But that's too much trouble."

"It won't be anything special. My father likes to meet young people. Can you?"

"Yes, if you're sure it's all right."

"Father will be honored."

"Do you like coffee?"

"Sometimes, if it isn't too strong."

"Would you like to have a cup of coffee with me?"

"Yes."

I took her to a fancy cafe in the neighborhood, telling myself there wasn't anything wrong with what we were doing. We didn't look at each other all the while we walked and talked, with me doing most of the talking. Her constant nodding made me uncomfortable.

When we came to the cafe Michiko stuck her head through the doorway as if to make sure the place was respectable. "Is this all right?" I asked. She hesitated for a second, then said yes.

The dark cafe was the kind of place where you would ordinarily sit with one cup of coffee for hours, for, as Mori used to say, you were paying for the rent. But we drank our coffee quickly and hurried out. I'd never felt so young in a public place, and Michiko did look like a girl in a middle school. We were also afraid we might run into someone we knew, and Michiko insisted on paying for her cup of coffee.

"Won't you let me pay for this?" I asked.

"You must let me pay for mine," she said seriously.

"Why?"

"Mother would be angry with me if I accepted a treat."

I let her pay for her share. At least she didn't say her mother wouldn't approve.

Michiko lived in a big rambling house on the outskirts of Tokyo where most of the houses had a lot of land and trees around them. It was quiet there, away from the city noise, and a little gloomy. A housemaid greeted us in the dark porch and laid out a pair of house slippers for me, and led us through the seemingly empty house. There was something eerie about the stillness of the place, the kind of place where you unconsciously lowered your voice, as in a hospital. We went up a flight of stairs and entered a spacious, elegant room, with an alcove in the corner where an old scroll was hanging. There were four or five oil paintings on the walls and I knew at least one of them was a work of a great painter. Next to the alcove was a rack that held three samurai swords with lacquered scabbards. But the thing that really caught my attention was a pair of *kotos* lying side by side on the floor. A *koto* is a kind of large Japanese zither with thirteen silken strings.

"Chie, a pot of tea, and please tell Sister we're here," said Michiko to the maid. The maid bowed and shuffled out of the room. It was strange to see Michiko lording it over a grown woman.

"Do you play?" I pointed at the *kotos.*

"I only pluck at it; my sister is the expert. I've always wanted to study the violin, but Father thinks *koto* is more ladylike. It must be wonderful for you to be able to study with your master."

"Yes, I'm very lucky; my parents don't object. But I don't see why you can't study the violin if you really want to. Can't you take lessons without telling your father?"

"No, I can't do that. I'm only a girl."

That's what they all say. I'm only a girl. There isn't much you can say to that, and I never knew whether it was a complaint or envy.

"I'll probably take it up some day," she said, "and find out I have no talent for it."

"I like music," I told her.

"I do, too. Classical music. Do you?"

I nodded and looked around the room. Two framed photographs on the writing table caught my eye. They were old-fashioned photographs, slightly yellowing; one was of a man in a white military uniform with medals on his chest, and the other was of a boy about my age, with hair cropped short, wearing a school uniform.

"That's my father." Michiko pointed to the man. "He was an admiral. It's been a family tradition with us. My grandfather was also an admiral."

Her father did look like an admiral, with an impressive handlebar mustache, holding a sword as casually as one would hold a walking cane.

"And that is my older brother. He would be twenty-three this year. He died right after the war."

I wanted to say something but the maid came in with the tea things. She was followed by a young woman in a flowered kimono.

The woman was about twenty, and looked beautiful with faint makeup.

"So you are Sei-san," she said and bowed. "I'm Yoko, Michi's sister. We've heard some fascinating things about you, so we know a little more about you than you know about us. It isn't fair, is it?"

I didn't know whether she was flattering or teasing me.

"You're embarrassing Sei-san." Michiko frowned at her sister.

"I'm sorry." Yoko smiled.

We sat on silk pillows and talked over tea and cakes. I was glad when Michiko asked her sister to play the piece she'd been practicing.

"My playing is only an amateur's delight," Yoko said politely and played the long instrument.

She was very good. The beautiful haunting air made me think of my childhood, when there was hardly any Western music. The sound of old Japan.

After the solo, Michiko joined her sister and they played a duet. Their father entered the room so quietly I wasn't aware of him until I heard the rustling sound of a kimono and saw him sit next to me. I started to bow but he raised his hand, signaling me to be still. He sat with his back straight, like a samurai lord, and listened to the music with his eyes closed. He was an impressive man, with white hair and a huge mustache.

"Welcome to my humble home," he said when the music came to the end. He had a great bass voice. "You must forgive Michiko's mother for not joining us. She's been ill for quite some time, and even a recital like this would be too taxing for her."

"I'm sorry, sir."

"It's one of those strange ailments that no one seems to know anything about. How did you like the music? They're rather good, don't you think?"

We hadn't been introduced but it didn't seem necessary.

"Yes, I think they're wonderful," I replied.

"You like Japanese music then?"

"Yes, sir, especially *koto* music."

"I think our music has more of a soul than Western music."

"But Father," said Yoko, "you've never listened to a live symphony. Sei-san, you mustn't pay much attention to Father. He's so old-fashioned, he won't even see a movie."

"I say what does a movie have over a good stage play? Noh and puppet plays are more my pace. But then what do we old men know? I understand you're a classmate of Michiko's."

"Yes, since the new term," I said, trying not to look at Michiko. She had lied to her father, and that pleased me. He would be a hard man to lie to.

"Father," said Yoko, "Sei-san is a pupil of Noro Shinpei."

"So I understand. It's hard to believe that Michiko and Sei-san are the same age. Why, he appears to be a grown man next to her."

"That's not fair, Father," said Michiko. "Sei-san is the tallest boy in school. He's taller than most of the teachers."

"Samurais of old were tall men. Height is a great advantage. You must take up kendo, Sei-san; you'd make a superb swordsman. We Japanese don't drink enough milk. How about some refreshments?"

Seeing me puzzled, Michiko said, "Father means sake. Will you have some?"

"Tea is fine for me, thank you," I said.

"Come, come, a little sake is a good thing. Why, in the old days men your age were sent into battle with nothing more than sake in their veins," he said and clapped his hands twice. The maid entered silently.

"Chie, warm some sake for us, four cups, and something to go with it."

We drank sake and he told us war stories. I'd heard a lot of war stories, but never from an admiral. His stories were fascinating, and he was a fine storyteller. He talked about Manchuria, the South Seas, even about America, where he was once a military attaché, and about the fabulous warships he'd commanded.

Perhaps because of my poor circulation sake never made my face turn red, and that impressed the admiral. He was the kind of man who judged other men by how much sake they could drink. I was relieved when the maid finally served our supper.

Michiko insisted that she see me off to the station, asking the maid to come after her in fifteen minutes. As we walked down the wide hallway I heard a door open behind me. I looked back and saw an ashen face of an old woman behind a partly opened door. The room was dark, and the woman's face stood out like a Noh mask, white and ghostly. Our eyes met briefly, then the door closed without a sound. I looked away quickly, realizing it was Michiko's mother.

Michiko and I walked on the deserted street, she casting a pool of light in front of us with a flashlight.

"Are you angry with me?" she asked.

"Why should I be angry? You mean about our being in the same class?"

"That, too, but for not warning you about Father's drinking. And Mother."

"No, of course not. He doesn't drink any more than Sensei. I think your father is wonderful."

"You saw my mother, didn't you?"

"She looks very ill."

"You see, she's never been the same since my brother died. She hasn't left her room in six years."

"She's been grieving all this time?"

"It's a long story. I don't know if I should tell you . . . my brother killed himself; he committed suicide when the war ended. He killed himself because he could never be an admiral like Father and Grandfather. I think my mother has gone mad — we can't even talk with her. It's been very hard on Father. Girls aren't quite the same as boys to a military man. He has often asked me to invite boys to the house. He likes to talk to young men, but I've never asked anybody before. I thought you would understand."

"How old was your brother?"

"Sixteen."

I didn't know what to say to her. We walked in silence.

"You aren't drunk, are you?" Michiko asked.

"I'm all right. . . . No one at school knows this, but I live alone."

"What do you mean?"

"I live alone in an apartment. My parents are divorced."

"How terrible for you!" She stopped in the middle of the street. "I can't imagine such a thing. Do you have to do your own cooking?"

I laughed. "I eat out. And I wash my own underwear. You shouldn't think your family is so strange — at least you're together."

As we continued our walk, I told her about my parents and Grandmother. Gently she touched my hand, I squeezed her small hand, and she tightened her grip in answer. No one had held my hand since I was a small boy, and something like a lost memory came rushing back to me. Holding hands with her seemed like the most natural thing to do; I longed to walk like that through the night, not saying a word. If I reminded Michiko of her dead brother, I didn't mind.

Coming near the station we saw the dark forms of people and we unclasped our hands and walked a few paces apart.

"I'm very glad you came," said Michiko.

"Should I wait until the maid comes?" I asked her.

"No, please go now."

"Good night then."

"I hope you'll come again."

"I'd like that very much; I'd be honored."

FIFTEEN
❖ ❖ ❖ ❖ ❖

After that I visited Michiko about once a month. The gloom in her house depressed me, and I felt tense, but her father seemed to enjoy my company. My visits were all alike: *koto* music, a few cups of sake, and supper that looked like it was ordered from a restaurant. Michiko was a good friend and I liked her. I wished I didn't think any more about Reiko, but I did.

Michiko was a straight A student, and that had an effect on me; I began to study harder. Once I stole a board that Sensei had discarded and gave it to Michiko. Tokida had done some of the background but I lied and told her it was all my work. She was delighted, and said she would have it framed.

A month before summer vacation I received a letter from my father. I was very surprised, because I hadn't heard from him in a long time. The first thing I saw in the envelope was a postal check for a large sum of money. I knew something had happened. This is what the letter said.

Koichi,

I trust that all is well with you. Enclosed is a money order which you may spend in any way you wish. Let me explain what has happened since I wrote to you last.

Do you remember Captain Powers, the American officer for whom I used to do translations? He has left the service and now resides in California. As you know we had become quite good friends, and we have kept in touch over the years. He wrote me last week and kindly offered to sponsor me and my family to emigrate to America, and I have accepted. I have already begun the paperwork from this end. I have been told that the process will take about a year, which will give me ample time to sell our house and my business.

Captain Powers remembers you well, and has asked about you. And, of course, when I say my family you are naturally included. So my question: Would you consider going with us? And should you decide to do so I must know as soon as possible, for there would be additional paperwork to be processed. I realize this is rather sudden notice, and if you would like to think things over, do so. I will be happy if you decide to join us, and needless to say I will be responsible for your education, lodging, etc. I suggest that you talk to your mother about it, but let me stress the point that the decision is ultimately yours. Do let me know soon.

Father

I was dumbfounded. I'd known about Father's wish to leave Japan, but I never thought he would actually do it. And it seemed ironic that my father chose to emigrate to a country that was our enemy only a few years before. I remembered the fair-haired American army captain who used to come to our house with candies and Coca-Cola and patiently teach me the English alphabet. But the strange thing about Father's letter was that he was giving me a choice, not an order. Perhaps our long separation had made him a little timid, or perhaps he'd given me the choice out of fatherly obligation whether or not he really wanted me to go with him. I read the letter over and over, trying to read between the lines, but that only confused me. It wasn't something I could decide overnight. I wrote to Father and asked him to give me time to think things over. First, I had to talk with Mother.

The idea of going to America did excite me. I thought of the skyscrapers, cars zooming at incredible speed on cloverleaf highways, cowboys and Indians, gangsters with machine guns, Gary Cooper and Humphrey Bogart. Maybe I should quit school immediately and take a crash course in English conversation.

But leaving Sensei and Tokida would be more painful than I cared to think about. And Motner would be 6,000 miles away. *This is a dog. No, it is a cat.* That was about the extent of my English. They would make me go through schooling all over again once I got to America. I wasn't ready to go back to an elementary school.

I decided to consult Sensei before going to Mother with the news. I took some of the best charcoal drawings I had done at school so we'd have something to talk about if our conversation bogged down and went to the inn.

"You did these?" asked Sensei. I nodded. "Pin this one up."

It was wonderful to watch Sensei study a drawing. He really looked at it. It was like watching someone eating a ripe peach.

"Superb," he declared. "I see you've been working very hard indeed. Here, pin the others up. What do you think, Tokida?"

"He's getting pretty good," he agreed. "I like that statue, the discus thrower. Maybe we ought to have one here, Sensei. I think Kiyoi should have drawn in the background, though."

"I agree," said Sensei. "Start putting in the background, Kiyoi. It's time you started paying attention to composition. Even if you only blacken the background, the drawing will stand out more. Do you find drawing nudes easier now?"

"A little, Sensei. It's so different from drawing plaster casts."

"They go hand in hand. You're concerned with shading in drawing the casts, but in life drawing line is the thing. Look at those beautiful grays. I'm impressed. Show me more, show me your sketchbooks."

While Sensei and Tokida looked over my drawings the kitchen

maid brought in a pot of tea and some sweets. I was glad for the interruption, because Sensei's praise and Tokida's silence made me nervous.

"Excellent," said Sensei. "I have only one thing to say for now, and it may not be all that important. Taikan, the great painter, once said that whenever he couldn't muster a technique, he would go with his heart. You don't seem to have that problem. You're blessed with extraordinary dexterity and I get a feeling that I'm being seduced by your cleverness. Look at her leg, for instance." He pointed at one of the nudes. "You're drawing like Matisse. It's quite beautiful, really, but I feel you weren't really looking at her leg when you drew it, but drew it the way you thought her leg *ought* to look. It's important that you don't seduce yourself with your own talent. Do you see what I'm getting at?"

He was right, of course. With Sensei, you couldn't get away with anything.

"Do I hear you arguing silently?"

"I was thinking about something else, Sensei. My father is going to America."

"For a visit?"

"No, he's emigrating. He asked me if I want to go with him. Do you know he has a new family now?"

"Yes, Tokida told me about your parents."

Tokida looked up.

"Well, are you going with him?" asked Sensei.

"I don't know. I wanted to talk to you first. I haven't told Mother yet. What do you think, Sensei?"

"*Wonderful*," he said in English.

"What do you want to go to America for?" asked Tokida. He sounded hostile.

"I don't know. I didn't say I was going."

"Let your beloved child journey," Sensei quoted an old saying. "When you have a chance to travel, travel. Traveling is the greatest teacher of all."

"So when is your old man going?" asked Tokida.

"In about a year, he said."

"You have some time to think about it then," said Sensei. "Even if you don't go with him now, he can always sponsor you later, am I right?"

"I guess you're right, Sensei. I never thought about that."

"Once you go there, then what?" asked Tokida. "Are you going to come back?"

"Sure I'll come back. I'll come back just to see you."

"You're not going to like it there, I tell you. You're a fool if you think America is such a special place. And you're not going to like their food."

"They have rice in America," I said, though I wasn't sure if that was true.

"According to Soseki," said Sensei, "salad was the only esthetic dish he found in Europe. But put your mind to rest, Kiyoi, we'll send you a monthly package. Rice crackers, soy sauce, dried squid, and ink. Our ink is the best in the world, I'll have you know, the blackest black ink you can find anywhere. All right, let's get to work. Kato is coming over early tomorrow morning."

We went to work. Sensei and Tokida seemed instantly to forget what I had told them about America. I knew Sensei wasn't the kind of man who showed his feelings freely, but still I was disappointed in his reaction. I wanted some kind of guidance, some comfort and sympathy; after all, it wasn't every day one had to make a decision like mine. But what he'd said about my going to America *after* my father came to me as a relief. I didn't feel so bad about stalling for time.

For the next three hours we didn't say much to one another, but worked furiously, Sensei handing us a board the minute he was through inking the main characters. That was all he did now, inking the main characters and the balloons. Tokida and I did the rest. We put in very ornate backgrounds, trying to outdo each other. When a board was finished, every frame on it looked like a fine book illustration, and even Sensei had a hard time telling who had drawn what.

After inking eight boards, Sensei left for the evening, trusting us to finish the rest. He did that more and more, especially on weekends. At suppertime the maid brought us a tray of Sunday feast.

"Do you think Sensei went straight home?" I asked.

"What do you mean?"

"You know, seeing someone instead of going home."

"You mean a mistress?"

"I don't know. Does he have a mistress?"

"How should I know? What he does is his business," said Tokida and lit a cigarette.

"I suppose so," I said. "A friend of mine at school thinks all artists have mistresses. Can I have one of your cigarettes?"

"Have you been smoking?" He stared at me, narrowing his eyes.

"Of course not. I want to see what it tastes like."

"So you draw like Matisse, and you think you're old enough to smoke."

"When did you start smoking?"

"When I was twelve, but that's different."

"Look, I'm never going to be as good as you, so give me a cigarette."

He tossed one from across the table. I picked it up and tapped it against the table and lit it.

"Don't take too big a drag, it'll choke you to death," he warned me.

I puffed at it a couple of times.

"Well?" he said.

"I don't feel a thing."

"Idiot, you didn't inhale it."

I took a mouthful of smoke into my lungs and felt a sharp stab and exploded in a coughing fit. Tears ran down my face and I felt dizzy and nauseated. Tokida reached over and took the cigarette, shaking his head. Actually I didn't feel that bad, but was acting for Tokida's sake. I had to humor him a little — showing him my drawings had been a mistake.

"A wonder boy," he said scornfully and shot something like a white rubber band at me. It fell on the floor next to me and when I picked it up I saw that it was a long elastic band with a small loop on each end.

111

"What's this for?" I asked.

"Something to hold my glasses on my head," he said without looking up.

"I never saw you wear it before."

"I only use it when I demonstrate."

"What? Do you mean to tell me you're still going to demonstrations?"

"You'd better keep it to yourself."

"You've been rioting all this time without telling me?"

"I don't have to tell you everything."

"What about your knife? Do you still have it?"

"Look, I told you I lost it."

"But why do you go to those riots?"

"Listen, I never asked you to come with me, did I? And stop calling them riots. They're demonstrations."

"You know something, Tokida? You're going to get hurt one of these days. You're asking for it."

"So who cares? You're going to America, and you can have your America. Me, I'm staying right here and I'm going to fight for what's right. This is my country. I'm not going anywhere. What I do is my business, and if I get hurt, that's my business too."

"I haven't decided if I'm going or not. But the next time you go to a demonstration, take me with you. It'll be safer if there are two of us. I didn't tell you before, but I've been taking karate lessons."

"What?"

"I've been taking lessons from the fellow I told you about who lives next door. He's going for his third-degree belt next month. He has the quickest hands I've ever seen. He's deadly."

"So you think you can fight the police with your bare hands? You think you can go against somebody with a knife, a stick even? Don't be a fool."

"I don't use my hands. I kick them in their shins and groins. Take me with you the next time — if you get in trouble maybe I can help."

"You don't know what you're talking about. Just worry about your America."

"Oh, hell, give me a cigarette."

"Go buy your own," he said and went back to work.

From now on I'll show him only my bad drawings, I promised myself.

SIXTEEN

❖ ❖ ❖ ❖ ❖

I thought of going to Yokohama to talk to Mother, but in the end I wrote to her instead. It was easier that way since I had no idea how she was going to react. I didn't say I wanted to go or not; I wanted to find out how she felt about it first. Mother replied immediately, saying how happy she was I had such an opportunity, that she would come to Tokyo in two weeks and we would talk things over at Grandmother's place. I wasn't eager to have Grandmother in on our conversation, but there was no way of getting around it.

It was early afternoon when I arrived. Mother was already there, and she and Grandmother were working away in the kitchen, preparing what looked like the New Year's feast. They had bought sea bream, large shrimps, and pickled melon from Nara, and were cooking rice with red beans in it. Red rice is cooked only on special occasions. Grandmother, having been pampered by servants most of her life, wasn't much of a cook, but neither was Mother. Grandmother was positively grinning the minute she saw me. Mother also seemed more high-spirited than usual.

"Sit, Koichi," ordered Grandmother. "Which would you rather have, tea or coffee?"

"Coffee? But you never keep coffee in the house. If it's American I'd like a cup, please," I said.

"The very best, Koichi," said Mother. "Today, you may have anything you wish."

"But I didn't make up my mind yet about going to America."

"Don't be fresh," said Grandmother. "Drink your coffee. Would you like cream with it?"

"Yes, please. Do you have condensed milk? And lots of sugar, please. So you want me to go to America, is that it?"

"We'll discuss that later," said Mother. "First things first."

"You mean this isn't my going-away party?"

"Look at him, Masako," said Grandmother. "He didn't tell me a thing."

"What didn't I tell you, Grandmother? Is the Empress pregnant?"

"Don't be disrespectful." Grandmother frowned. She was in an unusually good mood and I began to feel bolder.

"I know, you won the national lottery," I said.

"Don't talk rubbish. You know very well why we're celebrating," said Grandmother.

"I have no idea."

"You really don't know?"

"I swear by Buddha, Jesus Christ, Mohammed, whomever you like."

"That'll be enough, Koichi," said Mother. "Grandmother went to your school this morning."

"Oh?" I said, remembering the PTA meeting that morning.

"Do you remember," said Grandmother, "the first time I went to one of your school meetings? When I had to go through your exam papers with all the other parents present? You were near the bottom of your class, remember that? I wanted to crawl into a hole, Koichi, I'd never felt so humiliated in my life." I nodded, remembering it all too well.

"You are first in your class," said Grandmother. I looked at her

115

in surprise. "There's a girl in another class who scored two more points than you, but Mr. Sato told me that was because the girls have to take one class more than the boys. Home economics, I think. Nakano somebody."

Grandmother was talking about Michiko and that was no surprise. But the fact that I was first in my class did surprise me. I knew I had done well, but not that well.

"Are you sure, Grandmother? You weren't looking at someone else's papers, were you?"

"Of course I'm certain. Mr. Sato personally handed me your papers, and I had on my new glasses. After all, yours isn't a common name."

I looked at Mother but she turned away. I didn't know if Grandmother's comment about my name was intentional, but I felt a sudden anger swell up inside me. I felt she was still punishing Mother after all those years for marrying Father.

"What about America?" I changed the subject.

"What do you think, Mother?" Mother passed the question to Grandmother.

"I say he's too young, much too young. Why, he hasn't even finished middle school. He should at least finish high school here."

"But Mother, the longer he waits the more difficult it's going to be for him to learn English."

"But what is going to happen to his own language? After all he *is* Japanese. Do you suppose he's going to remember his middle school Japanese for long? Who knows what kind of schools they have in America. There's nothing like a well-educated man, and besides, only farmers emigrate to America. After all the sacrifices you've made to put Koichi in a good school, I think it's a pity."

All the sacrifice! She sounded as if I were the *only* one Mother had to worry about.

"Do you want me to go or not?" I asked Mother, not looking at Grandmother.

"That's not for me to say, Koichi," Mother replied. "Of course we'll miss you if you decide to go, but the decision is entirely up to you."

I was sure Mother was noncommittal because of Grandmother. I would have to talk to her alone. I was back where I had started.

❖ ❖ ❖

It was summer once again. I felt unsettled and irritable. Father's now frequent letters, urging me to make up my mind, didn't help, and neither did Tokida's absence from the inn; on days we didn't have much work, he was probably involved in riots, but as he said, that was his business. He and I seemed to be drifting apart. I didn't know what to do about it, and didn't much care. More and more I lost myself in painting and drawing, and also spent a good deal of time on my karate lessons.

My chest and arms had filled out somewhat during the year and I could go through some *katas* now. A *kata* is a kind of shadow boxing that one practices without a partner. The various movements of karate are combined in it so if you go through it properly it seems as though you're doing an elegant ceremonial dance. I was beginning to do some of the more complicated *katas*. So I was quite surprised when a few days after my fifteenth birthday, Mr. Kubota asked me to join him for supper after a late workout. I was still a rank novice, and being asked to supper by Mr. Kubota was like being invited to join the fraternity of experts.

"You're doing very well," he told me. "Two more years and I'll bet you'll be wearing a black belt."

His kindness embarrassed me. I remembered how stern he had seemed that first day I'd watched him instructing, and yet he never once shouted at me, nor said one unkind word, though once he'd blocked my punch during a mock fight and my arm had been bruised for days.

He took me to a Korean restaurant in a back alley of the Ginza and we each ordered the house special, strips of marinated meat cooked over a charcoal brazier right on our table.

I told him about my chance to go to America.

"That's exciting! When are you going?" he asked.

"If I decide to go I'll be leaving sometime next summer. Right now I don't know what I'm going to do."

"But what's there to decide?"

"If you had the chance, would you go?"

"Absolutely. A chance to get out of an island nation like ours and go live on a continent, I wouldn't think twice about it. We don't understand what it is to live with a lot of land around us."

"But I don't speak English. I'll have to start all over again."

"That won't be a problem. How old are you?"

"Fifteen."

"But that's so young. You'll pick up English in no time. Staying in this country for the rest of your life is like being a frog in a well. Think of your career."

He went on and on. It was good to hear such encouragement.

"I've been reading those books you lent me, *The Thibaults*." I changed the subject.

"Formidable undertaking. Martin du Gard won a Nobel Prize for that work. How far along are you?"

"I'm almost finished."

"I'm impressed. What do you think?"

"I don't understand some parts of it."

"For instance?"

"Do you remember where the older brother is thinking about his mistress after he gets a letter from her? He reads the letter, the letter that smells of her perfume, and he throws it away because he never keeps letters. But she wasn't just anybody. Then he says to himself that the woman is going to leave him someday soon. I mean he's so casual about it, so cool."

"Is that so unusual?"

"But how can you be in love and think about the day it's going to end?"

"I see what you're getting at," he said and paused for a second. "Don't you think that love has its own seasons?"

"What do you mean?"

"What I mean is that everything has a certain life cycle — a beginning, a middle, and an end — like a work of literature. Isn't that so?"

"Are you saying that love is the same way? What about art then? Is there an end to art?"

"Is there an end to life?" he countered with a question. I wasn't used to that kind of discussion, and somehow his question didn't seem fair.

"Anyway," he said, "the man you're talking about is a worldly man who's had many lovers. He's carrying on an affair with a woman who he knows will leave him some day. So he throws the letter away, a symbolic gesture. It simply means that he's looking at the situation with a good deal of detachment; he's seeing a pattern in all the love affairs he'd had in the past. Do you know that some men go through so many women they actually tire of women? Do you know that many men go after young boys?"

"Yes, I know, I've read about that. But Mr. Kubota, do you think women have feelings like men?"

"Do they love as we do? Is that what you mean?"

"Yes, I suppose so," I said, and felt my ears turning red.

"I think what you're trying to find out is whether there is such a thing as love. I'd like to think there is, though it may turn out to be something quite different from what we expect. For instance, I don't expect to find love in my marriage."

"You don't?"

"Not at all. No doubt my parents will choose my future wife and I'll probably be very happy with the arrangement."

"You mean you're going to have mistresses?"

"Why not?"

I didn't know what to say to that. Van Gogh had loved only one woman and that seemed like the natural thing to do. But the woman he loved had no love to give him. Perhaps he was unlucky. But then maybe all love affairs were like that, one-sided love the Japanese call the abalone love, for an abalone has only one shell. I'd been feeling like an abalone for quite some time.

It was drizzling when we left the restaurant. Mr. Kubota opened his umbrella and held it over our heads. He was always careful with his immaculately pomaded hair.

"There's an interesting cabaret near here," he said. "Let me buy you a drink to celebrate your good fortune."

"I'd like that," I said eagerly as we turned into a narrow street full of drinking places.

"Have you ever been here?" he asked me, pointing to a fancy nightclublike place with a thick glass door in front and a blue neon sign above an awning. I shook my head and he led me up the carpeted staircase. What an odd thing to ask, I thought. Did he think I frequented such a place? Then perhaps he was being polite, treating me like an adult.

It was a bar, a dark and crowded place, hazy with smoke. Men and women sat around tables cluttered with gleaming cocktail glasses. They were all silhouetted against the bar that looked like a brightly lit stage at the end of the long narrow room; it was like walking into a dark Daumier painting. A hostess in a kimono seated us at a table with four chairs. And no sooner had we sat down than two hostesses, also wearing kimonos, appeared out of the dark and joined our table. The place was full of hostesses. Mr. Kubota didn't seem in the least annoyed by the intrusion; he smiled and said something to them and the women giggled, covering their mouths with their hands. Obviously Mr. Kubota was an old hand at teasing bar women. I couldn't even look them in the eye. One of them pushed her chair and sidled up to me and I automatically moved away from her. She wore a strong perfume and smoked a cigarette in a black holder.

"What will you have?" asked Mr. Kubota.

"I don't know. What are you going to have?"

"A whiskey sour. Will you have one?"

"I'll try it."

"Two whiskey sours," said the hostess next to me and left the table to get our drinks. Mr. Kubota seemed calm and relaxed, draping his right arm over the backrest of the other hostess's chair. The woman leaned over and whispered in Mr. Kubota's ear and they laughed like old friends. I had a feeling that her comment was about me.

The hostess returned with four glasses on a tray; apparently they were having whiskey sours also. And as she sat down she touched my glass with hers and smiled. She was rather pretty. The drink was awful. It was my first whiskey and it tasted harsh and medicinelike.

"Are you Kubota-san's classmate?" she asked me. She even knew his name.

"How old do you think he is?" Mr. Kubota asked before I could answer. The women studied me.

"Nineteen? Twenty?"

"Very close," he said. "He's just finishing high school. He's quite an artist besides being a good karate man."

"How nice," said the woman on my side and looked at me with something like admiration in her eyes. It was hard to tell if they believed him, and if they didn't, they were certainly good actresses. The dim lighting made everything and everybody seem unreal, mysterious, ageless.

"What sort of art do you do?" asked Mr. Kubota's companion.

"Mostly drawings," I said without looking at her.

"He's being modest," said Mr. Kubota. "His drawings are no ordinary drawings. He's the star pupil of the great Noro Shinpei."

"The cartoonist?" she asked.

"The very same."

It was a relief not to have to do the talking. Mr. Kubota was probably trying to put me at ease.

"Show me your hand," said the hostess beside me. "Let me see the hand of an artist." She took my left hand in hers and began to stroke it. I pulled back, almost jerking it away, feeling nervous and uncomfortable. Mr. Kubota watched me with an amused look on his face. The woman laughed and took out a package of cigarettes from inside her kimono and offered it to me. I shook my head, but the other hostess reached out and took one. Mr. Kubota was quick with the match. The bartender put a new record on the phonograph and Mr. Kubota asked his companion to dance, and the two of them joined the other couples in the narrow aisle. It was weird to watch hostesses in flowered kimonos clinging to men in business suits, shuffling mindlessly to loud music with a saxophone blaring. I couldn't see what pleasure those men found in dancing with hostesses, especially Mr. Kubota, who was magnificent when he was doing a difficult karate dance but on the dance floor looked clumsy and out of place.

"You don't dance?" asked the hostess.

"No," I said, almost in a panic.

"It's easy, you know." She tilted her head to one side and peered into my eyes.

"No, I couldn't do it."

"Don't worry, I won't force you." She laughed, and reached out for a cigarette and put it into her holder. I struck a match to light it for her, and as she put the cigarette to the flame her face glowed in the small orb of light. My heart gave a violent thump — I saw dark roots of whiskers protruding through the thick layer of face powder. Noticing me staring, she quickly blew out the match and the cloud of smoke and the darkness hid her face from me. I stole a quick glance at her profile and saw a big Adam's apple. Her hand on the table had long painted nails, but her veins were too thick. She was a man! I felt a chill down my spine and my head reeled; my body went stiff with loathing. I sat up straight in my chair and pretended to watch the dancers, hoping desperately for the music to stop.

When Mr. Kubota and his partner finally returned to the table, I stood up, nearly upsetting the glasses.

"The toilet is in the back of the bar," the dancing hostess told me. For the first time I noticed the strange throaty quality of *her* voice, almost like the voice of a ventriloquist. She picked up the long butt she'd left in the ashtray; she *also* had thick veins on her hands.

"I have to go," I said. "I'm sorry. I remembered something I have to do."

"But we just got here," said Mr. Kubota. "You haven't even finished your drink."

"I have to go now, really. I'm sorry."

Mr. Kubota looked up at me with a faint smile. I looked away quickly.

"What's the matter? One drink isn't going to do your head in, is it?" he said teasingly.

"It isn't that, really; I just remembered something."

"How naughty of you, rushing off like this. I wanted to read your palm," whined the one who had fondled my hand.

"Oh, well, if you must go, then you must go. Here I'll finish your drink." Mr. Kubota reached for my glass.

"I'd like to pay for my drink," I said.

"Don't be silly. It's my treat, remember? And I'm drinking it," he said and gave me a searching look.

"Thanks. I'm sorry, really," I said and struggled around the table. From the corner of my eye I saw him drawing on his companion's cigarette. I'd never seen him smoke before.

I was grateful he didn't leave with me. Faces turned to look at me as I went down the aisle and I knew they were all men, every one of them. I staggered down the staircase, pushed open the heavy glass door, and threw up in the gutter. A young couple stopped and stared at me with disgust. "Sorry," I whispered, and covering my mouth with a handkerchief I rushed out of the narrow alley. It was still drizzling and the neon signs and shop lights glowed on the wet black pavement. My steps echoed against the hard and solid asphalt, but I felt as though I was gliding on a thin surface of two strange worlds — one of them upside down. I felt as if the ground under me would give way any minute, that I would plunge into the wild maze of reflections. And I wanted to fall, fall deep into the earth and never come up again. I stood next to a kiosk, staring blankly into the subway entrance, a gaping hole in the ground with bright light shining from the inside. I went under.

The damp still air and the chalky light of the fluorescent lamps comforted me. Walking deeper into the tiled tunnel I made a mental note of the place: If I ever found myself in a situation where I had no place to sleep, this would be a good place to come. Here, you would never know if it was raining outside, and night and day were all the same.

The sleepy-looking man behind the ticket window sold me a ticket without looking up. I stood on the empty platform and gazed absentmindedly at the DANGER! sign on the other side of the rails. The sign warned me of the electrified rails. If people are stupid enough to touch the rails, then let them be electrocuted, I thought. A train came roaring in with a blast of lukewarm air. It was nearly empty. I went in and stood by the automatic door, watching the concrete wall begin to streak, then turn into a dark blur, as the train began to move faster.

I got off at Asakusa, the end of the line. The rain had stopped, so I wandered down the cobblestone street that leads to a famous shrine where people from all over Japan came to ask for their wishes. The stores and shops were shut for the night and I was glad of the darkness and gloom. I roamed through the back alleys of the district until I was completely lost.

A single red light of a police box burned at the end of the alley, and a lone policeman stood still like a statue in front of the box. As if I had done something wrong, I skirted around the policeman and entered a wide street with inns crowding in on both sides. The street seemed unusually bright and noisy for that time of the night, and I realized that I was in the heart of Yoshiwara, the most famous pleasure quarter in all of Japan. A place princely warlords and noblemen, as well as samurais and common laborers, had frequented for as long as the old Edo had been the nation's capital. I started to turn back toward the police box.

"Want some fun, young fellow?" a prostitute called from a doorway.

"What's the hurry, Brother? Come inside, there's nothing better down the street," said another and cackled. I looked straight ahead and walked hurriedly, sidestepping a drunk on the way. Two kimono-clad women blocked my way.

"Say, Big Brother, what's the rush?" said one, smelling of sake and perfume.

"Come on, good-looking, let me take care of you," said the other, seizing me by the arm.

"Let go of me, please," I pleaded.

But the women just laughed and began to pull me toward a brightly lit doorway. At first I thought they were joking, but they were stronger than I'd expected. My God, they're going to drag me inside whether I like it or not, I thought. Gripped with fear, I began to struggle. They're going to take me inside and strip me and rob me, I thought in a panic. I grasped the wrist of the woman on my left, and squeezed hard.

"My, you're strong! You brute," mocked the woman. She had a pimple on her forehead. I looked at her neck to see if she had a big Adam's apple. She was a woman, all right, but not much to look at. The other woman was shorter and had her eyelids painted black with greasy paint.

"Please let me go; I don't want to hurt you," I said to them.

"Hurt us?" They started to cackle. "We want to give you a good time, silly."

"What's going on?" shouted a short stocky man in a *happi* coat, coming out of the doorway. "Is he giving you trouble? What are you doing with a boy?" His thick forearms were covered with tattoos.

"It's all right, Hatchan; we can take care of him," said the taller one.

"See, Big Brother, there's no use fighting us. Be nice and I'll make you feel good," said the short one.

Suddenly I wished that Mr. Kubota had been with me. This was worse than being in a room full of painted men. And why wasn't that policeman patrolling the street? Maybe I should kick the women in their shins and run. I knew I could easily disable them with a couple of swift blows, but what about the mean-looking lout inside the doorway? Could I take care of him with a kick in his groin? Maybe the policeman would come running if I shouted loud enough. While all this was going through my mind the two women continued to drag me toward the inn. I was about to use karate for the first time when I heard a voice behind me.

"Let go of him." It was an order. I turned my head and saw Sensei.

"I said let go of him!" he said again in a low hiss. The women dropped my arms and stepped back.

"Well!" the one with the pimple said in a miffed voice.

"A friend of yours, I suppose," said the other.

"That's right. Now, go on," said Sensei.

"Why don't you keep him off the street then? He doesn't look old enough to shave," said the short prostitute.

"Let's get out of here, Kiyoi," said Sensei.

As we walked in silence down the middle of the street, I kept thinking that Sensei hadn't had to show himself to me in a place like that, that he could have gone the other way and left me to fend for myself. A few prostitutes called to us but we paid no attention and they didn't come near us. At the edge of Yoshiwara, Sensei hailed a taxi, and we sped through the dark, deserted streets of Tokyo.

"Sensei," I started to say.

"No need to explain, Kiyoi. Let's just say we were out for a little social study," he said.

"Yes, sir."

When I got out in front of my apartment, Sensei rolled down the window and said, "Kiyoi, sometimes a little social study is a good thing for us artists. You *are* an artist, remember that."

"Yes, sir."

"Get a good night's sleep," he said and ordered the driver to head toward Takata-no-Baba.

SEVENTEEN

❖ ❖ ❖ ❖ ❖

After the incident at the bar I avoided Mr. Kubota for a time, but in the end I went back to the gymnasium. Besides being a good teacher, he was my neighbor, and, as Tokida would say, whatever he did on his own was his business. And for his part, Mr. Kubota acted as if nothing had happened, so I continued to take lessons from him, though not as often as before.

I was quite surprised one Saturday morning in September, when Sensei came to see me. He seemed distressed, his eyes were bloodshot, and his face bristled with heavy stubble. Through the doorway I could see a taxi parked with its motor running.

"I'm glad I found you at home," said Sensei, breathing heavily.

"What happened?" I asked anxiously.

"Quickly, get dressed. I'll tell you in the cab. Tokida's been hurt."

"Oh, no!"

"He's alive. Hurry!"

"What happened, Sensei?"

"It seems Tokida was in a riot."

"I knew it! How bad is he?"

"Not good, Kiyoi. Two broken ribs, a broken leg, and a concussion."

"Is he going to be all right?"

"He'll live. He may never walk properly, but the doctors don't think his brain was damaged. Thank God for that."

"You've seen him then?"

"A couple of hours ago. He asked about you — maybe you can cheer him up a little. Tell me, Kiyoi, how long has he been demonstrating?"

"I've been in only one of them, Sensei, sometime last summer. I think it was the first time he was in a riot. It was an accident. We were walking near Hibiya Park when we, well, sort of got sucked into it. Tokida said it was a protest march, but people went wild and we couldn't get out of it."

"Did he have a knife?" Sensei looked me straight in the eye.

"Did he kill somebody?" I asked in a whisper.

"Did he have a knife?" he asked again.

I nodded. "He said he was trying to protect me. . . . He said he lost it. He didn't have it after the riot," I said, almost in tears.

"They claim he stabbed a policeman in the thigh."

"Did they find a knife on Tokida?"

"That's just it, there is no knife."

"Then how can they accuse him?"

"I have no idea, except that Tokida was arrested near the wounded policeman. The police mentality has always been a mystery to me; I don't understand why they're accusing Tokida. The only thing I can think of is that they've checked up on his Osaka records and figured him to be the likely suspect. I wish he'd told me about those demonstrations," said Sensei and held his head in his hands.

"But he did tell you he didn't have a knife," I said.

"That's what he said."

"Then he didn't have it, and he didn't stab anybody. You have to trust him, Sensei. He does a lot of crazy things, but he'd never

128

lie to you. I know. I know how he feels about you. He'd lie to his own mother before he'd lie to you."

We were now in front of the hospital. Sensei looked at me steadily.

"All right, he didn't do it. I believe you, and I believe in Tokida. If they want to prosecute Tokida, they'll have to go through me, and I say there's no case here. Come, he wants to see you."

I had not been inside a hospital since I was a child, and all the horrors of the place came back to me — the dimly lit endless corridors, the soft clinking of hypodermic syringes and the cutting instruments, the sick on stretchers and in wheelchairs. And the smell of antiseptic and lab alcohol.

Not bothering to take the crowded elevator, we went up the staircase to the third floor and entered a large, long ward with a row of beds on both sides. Most of the beds were occupied, and those patients who weren't asleep looked up at us, as if hoping to see a familiar face. Some stared blankly at the ceiling. The sight of them made me want to talk to them, one and all, and run out and get cigarettes and magazines for them. I was alive and well, and glad of it.

Tokida lay flat on his back on the second bed from the end, near an open window. His head was wrapped in bandages covering the sides of his face. His right leg rested on top of the blanket and was in a cast up to his kneecap. He was smoking. When he spotted us he started to raise his body, then winced in pain and lay back. He gave me a faint smile and reached for his glasses on the side table. Tears welled up in my eyes.

"Hey, lie back, you fool," I said and kneeled beside his bed.

"Did you eat anything for lunch?" asked Sensei.

Tokida nodded faintly.

"How do you feel?" I asked.

He nodded again.

"Do you hurt?"

He shook his head. "I feel fine. Morphine," he whispered.

"That's good," said Sensei. "Try not to move. We came by to see how you were. I don't think it's good for you to talk, so we won't stay long. If you want anything we'll bring it tomorrow.''

Tokida shook his head.

"It's a good thing they didn't break your drawing hand," I said.

"Indeed, it's been hard enough teaching you to draw with your right hand," said Sensei.

Then we fell silent. I took the glass ashtray on the side table and emptied it. Tokida reached for another cigarette and I lit it for him. His hand shook slightly.

"Now there's a funny sight," said Sensei, leaning out the window. "There's a little boy down on the lawn blowing bubbles. The poor fellow is having a hard time keeping the bubbles away from the dog. The boy turns round and round, away from the dog, but the dog is too quick. Now he's pushing the dog and spilling soap all over the place. All gone. What frustration! The boy drops on the grass, time for a little tantrum. Hear him?''

Through the window we heard the child cry. Tokida chuckled.

"Sensei, I don't think it's good for Tokida to laugh," I said.

"Yes, quite. Let's be on our way, Kiyoi. Let Tokida rest a little. Don't worry about work, Tokida. Kiyoi will keep me company. We'll be back tomorrow.''

"Thank you for coming," whispered Tokida as we left the ward.

At the small shop on the first floor Sensei bought a tin of fifty cigarettes and a magazine and told me to take them up to Tokida. He was giving me a chance to be alone with Tokida. I rushed back to his bed. He had his glasses off again, and seemed surprised to see me.

"Here," I said and put the two things on the side table. He gave me a nod and put on his glasses. I kneeled beside his bed and looked him in the eyes.

"Did you do it?" I asked.

He seemed puzzled.

"Did you stab that policeman?"

His eyes widened. "No," he said.

"I knew you didn't. I told Sensei you didn't.''

"What are you talking about?"

"Didn't Sensei ask you about the knife?"

"He asked me if I had a knife and I told him no. What's going on anyway?"

"Don't you know? Didn't Sensei ask you about the policeman?"

"What policeman? What are you talking about? All I remember is Sensei asking me about the knife, and I told him I didn't have one."

"Never mind then," I said.

"No, tell me, what are they accusing me of?"

I told him.

"Fools," he hissed, clenching his teeth.

"Don't worry about it; it's all right now."

"Does Sensei think I'd do a thing like that?"

"No, of course not, it's all right, forget it. He was concerned because he spoke to the police first and only knew their version. It's all right now — he knows you didn't do it. He trusts you."

Tokida lit another cigarette and lay back.

"Do you hurt a lot?" I asked him.

He nodded and gave me a grin.

"But you're going to be all right. I'll see you tomorrow, Nisan," I said and left quickly.

That's what you call your older brother. I'd never called him that before, or anybody for that matter. It happened without my thinking and I was glad I had said it. More than anything I wanted him to be well again. I didn't ever want to draw better than Tokida.

EIGHTEEN
❖ ❖ ❖ ❖ ❖

The police dropped all charges against Tokida — insufficient evidence, they said. I didn't think the verdict surprised Sensei, but the news made him jubilant. He went out and bought a small keg of fine Kyoto sake and had a maid warm it up for us in our room. We laughed a lot that night, perhaps too much, trying to keep our spirits high, but our celebration wasn't complete without Tokida to share it with us.

I went to the hospital every day, and as Tokida regained his strength he became more talkative, but he never mentioned anything about the riot and I never asked. He felt bad about not being able to work, and probably felt a little jealous that I was doing all the work. He worried about his hand going rusty, so Sensei brought him a thick sketchbook and some soft-leaded pencils and soon Tokida was drawing his fellow inmates in the ward. He could draw anywhere, at any time — something I respected and envied. He was living the life of his hero, van Gogh, with his head wrapped in bandages, drawing like a madman. He had to stay in the hospital almost two weeks.

I thought a lot about Tokida while he was away. He never had any trouble making decisions: He would make up his mind about something, go out, and do it. I envied him. I was always mulling over things, until I'd be too confused to know what I was thinking. But now I *had* to make up my mind about going to America. And the best way I knew was to talk to Mother, alone, to find out how she felt about it. I decided to see her at her shop without warning her ahead of time so she wouldn't have time to prepare what she was going to say.

It was late afternoon when I got off the train at Yokohama. As I approached the shop I was seized with an uneasy feeling, and slowed down my pace. I hadn't really thought out what I was going to say to her.

I was a few doors down the street from the shop when I saw Mother come out. Before I could think, something made me duck quickly behind a telephone pole. She was accompanied by a man, and they were walking away from me. I crossed the street and followed them at a safe distance.

He was tall, perhaps even a little taller than I, and was wearing a dark topcoat that contrasted with Mother's light camel-colored coat. They were carrying on an animated conversation, and from time to time they looked at each other and laughed. I saw his profile. He had thick eyebrows and a big angular jaw. Suddenly I thought about my father and wished something I hadn't wished in a long time; I wished that things had been different, that my parents were still together. I wished that the man walking next to Mother had been my father.

They crossed an intersection, and when they came in front of a small cafe the man motioned to Mother to go inside. My watch said four-thirty-five. I decided to wait for them to come out, even if it took four hours. I browsed in the shops on the block, always keeping a sharp eye on the cafe door. Who is he? I wondered. What are they talking about? What are they drinking? Coffee? Maybe whiskey sours. Is he a business associate of Mother's? Should I go up to them when they come out and say hello?

The more I thought about these things, the more uneasy I felt. I was miserable, and yet I could not bring myself to leave. I bought an apple from a fruit vendor and took one bite, then threw the rest in a trash bin.

Forty-five minutes later they came out smiling at each other, and Mother nodded her head a couple of times to him. The man had probably paid for the drinks and she was thanking him. I felt my heart beat as I followed them. It was getting dark and the bright shop lights hurt my eyes. I put my coat collar up, to break the wind and to hide my face. The man held Mother's elbow lightly as they crossed the busy street, and hailed a taxi.

I stood there a long time, looking in the direction where the cab had disappeared in the traffic. I felt a heavy numbness in my head, and in my body. The ground under me seemed to have disappeared, and yet my body was heavy. I wished I hadn't come. What she did wasn't my business, but I didn't *have* to know about it. I tried to fool myself by thinking perhaps I had seen things, that I had made up the whole thing, but it was no use. The cold air stung my eyes and burned my cheeks; the chill cut right through my wool coat, and I felt it on my spine. The coldness was the only thing I truly felt, and in a strange way it comforted me. I walked in the darkening light, all the way to the train station.

Mother was thirty-six years old, but she didn't look it; she was beautiful. It was stupid to think that she didn't have a suitor. Would she marry him? Perhaps she was holding out because of Grandmother and me. Especially me. My schooling was expensive; my apartment was expensive. If I were out of the way, she'd be free to do whatever she pleased. I now had my answer.

I went home and wrote to Father. I would go with him to America.

❖ ❖ ❖

The day Tokida was released from the hospital, Sensei brought him home in a taxi, and we helped him up the staircase. Because of his broken ribs he couldn't use crutches, and had to limp around with a walking cane. He couldn't sit on the floor with the cast on his leg, so Sensei had the innkeeper bring up a tall office desk and a chair and set them up in a corner.

Later that afternoon when Sensei left for the evening I told Tokida of my decision.

"I'm going to America," I said. "I'll be leaving next summer."

Tokida said nothing.

"Well, what do you think?" I asked.

"What did Sensei say?"

"I haven't told him yet."

"So what's the big secret?"

"It's no secret. I wanted you to be the first to know."

"You're not going to like it there, I tell you. I'll give you two years and you'll be back. What made you decide all of a sudden?"

"I've been thinking about it for a long time."

"What's wrong with being a cartoonist here? I thought we would work together."

"Maybe we can do that anyway. I'm not going to the moon, Tokida. I might come back in a year or two and, who knows, maybe we can set up our own studio then."

"No, Kiyoi, once you go, that's it. You'll never be the same again. It's like my trying to go back to Osaka. You think things are better over there? Are you running away from something?"

"No, I'm not running away from anything."

"Why are you going then?"

"I don't know, Tokida. Maybe just to go to a new place. Don't you ever feel like that sometimes? Going to a foreign country and being a complete stranger?"

He looked at me steadily.

"I guess there's nothing wrong in that. I did it myself. You ought to do it then; I didn't know you felt like that. Sure, I know what you're saying, you want to be alone for a while, but I tell you, Kiyoi, don't stay there if things don't work out. You're not going to lose face by coming back. Do what you want to do and don't ever listen to anybody."

"No, I won't. . . . Will you tell Sensei about it? I don't want to tell him I'm going away."

"I'll tell him. It's probably better that way. You want a cigarette?"

"No, thanks."

"Don't worry about Sensei. I'll tell him."

"Thanks."

❖ ❖ ❖

I told Mother next, at Grandmother's house. She would never know how I had arrived at my decision. I felt like I was testing her, to see how she would react.

"You've made the right choice, Koichi," she said calmly. "It's a wonderful opportunity for you. I wanted you to go, for your sake, but I didn't want to influence you. We'll miss you, of course, but your future is more important."

Grandmother sat in silence.

"What do you think, Grandmother?" I asked.

"Will they treat you kindly?" she asked, leaning over the charcoal brazier to warm her hands.

"What do you mean?" I asked.

"We've been enemies, Koichi, and the war has been over for only a few years." Mother and I looked at her in amazement.

"It's all over, Mother," said Mother. "We're friends now. People don't go on being enemies forever."

"There are things people don't forget," said Grandmother.

"I can always say I'm a Korean," I suggested.

"Nonsense. You're no more Korean than I or your mother. You should be proud of your blood. Besides, look at what's happening in Korea. Koreans are their enemies now."

"Mother, it isn't as if Koichi fought in the war — he's only a boy," said Mother.

"That's just the problem. He's not old enough to fend for himself."

"But he is not going alone. He'll be with his father."

"What difference does that make?" Grandmother grunted. "His father! So you think he is going to be a responsible father all of a sudden; don't be naive, Masako. Has he ever been a good father? What has he ever done for Koichi? Has he ever helped pay for his education? He's done nothing, absolutely nothing. He's not of our blood; he's an outsider. I never trusted that man, and I never will."

"How can you say that?" I was taken aback by her bitterness. She'd never spoken like this in front of me before. "You don't even know him. You've never met my father."

"That'll be enough, Koichi," Mother cautioned me.

"That's the trouble with you, Masako," said Grandmother. "You're too softhearted. You've been too good for that man, and look what he's done to you. Men are all alike."

"Stop it, Mother; he's Koichi's father."

"I've said what I think."

"But I'm a man, Grandmother," I said. "At least I will be."

"You're my grandson," she said and closed her eyes. "There will be many hardships. You don't speak their tongue, and you're different from them. You don't know what it is to be different from everybody else. You don't even know what it is to be alone, to have no one to comfort you. But you're young, full of foolish ideas. . . . If you really want to go, then go. My grandson . . ." she said as if to herself.

I realized then that she wasn't only saying that she would miss me — she was thinking about her death, that our parting would be final. I never knew she cared for me that much.

"We must stop this right now. This is supposed to be a joyous occasion. I'll go and put the kettle on," said Mother and went to the kitchen.

Mother must be craving for a cigarette, I thought. Tokida would have gone mad without one by now. Though Mother never said much in front of Grandmother, I knew she was a woman of strong will. She was glad that I was going, for my sake, and I was glad to be out of her way. I wondered how long it would be before she would remarry.

Father began to send me a steady stream of letters, instructing me in the tedious business of getting my papers in order. At the beginning of February he wrote to say that he was coming to Tokyo for a few days, to be interviewed by the American Consul General, and also to take care of some business. He gave me the date of his arrival and the name of the hotel where he would stay, and asked me to reserve one day to spend with him. Now that my school knew I was leaving I was excused from classes almost at will.

A day after Father arrived I went to the big European-style hotel to meet him. I asked for him at the front desk and waited in the lobby. I felt nervous about meeting Father for the first time in more than four years. I tried to imagine what he would look like now, but the only picture that came to my mind was the look on his face as he'd slipped his gold watch off his wrist to give me when we'd parted.

In about five minutes Father came out of the elevator. He seemed shorter than I remembered. When he spotted me his face broke into a big grin. He hadn't changed much, though now there was more white than black in his hair.

"Don't tell me you're still growing," he exclaimed as he walked up to me. Father was always a little theatrical and his exhibitionism embarrassed me. Then he did a strange thing: He extended his right hand toward me and held it there. He meant for me to shake it, but I just stared at it, because it isn't customary for Japanese to shake hands. Finally, I took his hand and shook it meekly, and noticed how small his hand was, with short, stubby fingers. It was as if my father had shrunk since the last time I'd seen him.

"You haven't eaten, have you?" he asked. I shook my head. "Good, we're going to have a good lunch. You don't mind if my business associate joins us, do you?" he said, and before I could reply he grasped me by the arm and ushered me to the front desk.

"Meet my son," he said grandly to the clerk and handed him his room key.

"A fine-looking young man, sir," said the clerk and gave me a short bow.

We walked out into the cold. Like so many short men, Father had very good posture, and walked briskly. He reached out and pulled my left hand out of my coat pocket.

"Don't you have a pair of gloves?" he asked.

"I don't need them," I said.

"Try this." He removed a suede glove from his hand and gave it to me, but of course it was too small for me.

"What am I going to do with you? I bet you can't wear ready-made clothes anymore." Father looked embarrassed. "So what sport do you play?"

"I don't have much time for sports, Father."

"Not even soccer?"

"No, but I've been taking karate lessons."

"Ha!" he cried and took a leaping step ahead of me, then turned suddenly to face me, standing in a classic boxer's stance.

"Come, hit me!" he challenged with a mocking smile.

In his youth Father had been a professional boxer in Shanghai. I remembered the time when he had brought home two pairs of boxing gloves that an American soldier had given him. And with the heavy practice gloves he gave me my first boxing lesson. It wasn't much of a lesson — all he did was jab me in the face with his quick hands until my nose bled and I began to cry. My crying made him furious. He continued jabbing me until Mother came running out of the house to save me. My face was covered with blood and tears.

The same man now beckoned me teasingly with his raised fists. I was at least five inches taller than he, and with my long legs I could have kicked him in his groin and disabled him in an instant. I stared at him, not knowing whether to laugh or go through a mock fight with him. Then Father took a step and shot his left hand at my shoulder, to give me a tap, no doubt, a friendly gesture. I should have stood still, but automatically my right hand flew up to block his strike. It was pure reflex. Our forearms made contact, and the momentum of my strike sent his arm flying up in the air. The smile on his face disappeared.

"You're quick, aren't you?" he said and nudged my shoulder with his closed fist. I stood still this time. I wanted to apologize, but didn't. He did not like apologies.

He began to walk quickly once again, leading the way.

"What would you like to do this afternoon?" he asked.

"There are a lot of good movies," I said, not knowing what else to suggest.

"Let's see a movie then; you make the choice."

He took me to a well-known European restaurant where his associate joined us. We went through the usual introduction, his friend asking my age, commenting on my height. Father beamed with pride, grasping my arm and giving me a light punch on the shoulder. Then the two discussed business the rest of the time. Father ate like a Westerner, handling his knife and fork with ease. I tried to imitate him, though it was an awkward way to eat.

"So what's your plan for the afternoon?" asked his friend.

"I think we'll take in a movie. There are only two theaters where I live."

His friend made a clacking sound with his tongue in disapproval.

"A movie? Why not Nichigeki? Your son looks old enough for that sort of thing." He nodded at me with a knowing smile.

"Perhaps next time," said Father. "I think a movie is in order."

"Let me take you there before you leave Tokyo. You shouldn't miss the striptease theater; it's the best thing in town," he said.

I wished I hadn't said anything about movies — I felt I was wasting Father's time. But he seemed to enjoy the movie and it was a relief for me to sit in the dark theater and not have to talk for two hours.

When we came out of the theater Father looked at his watch and said, "I'd like to take you to dinner but I have a business engagement. Give me a call tomorrow and maybe we can spend a few hours together. Here . . ." He started to give me some money.

"I still have the money you sent me," I told him.

"Take it anyway. I want you to buy decent luggage, and have some clothes made, at least one suit."

I thanked him and stuffed the large bills in my pocket.

"I'm glad you're coming with me, son," he said, and grasped my right hand with both hands and squeezed hard.

I wanted to tell him that I was glad also, but all I could do was to nod to him awkwardly. He walked away quickly, without looking back. He's going to call his friend and they're going to see the striptease, I thought to myself.

NINETEEN

❖ ❖ ❖ ❖ ❖

To make clothes to take to America seemed silly, and as for the luggage I could easily fit everything I needed in one suitcase. I was planning to ask Mother to let me have the suitcase we used when we left Father; somehow it seemed right that I should take it on my long journey.

Time passed quickly. I left school at the end of May to prepare for my departure. There wasn't much to prepare — I just wanted some time to myself. Though I was to leave in the middle of the following month, I didn't believe that I was actually going, and yet I had a brand-new passport with my picture in it. I still had all the money Father had given me, and the check he'd sent me still lay in my desk drawer. I don't know why, but I hesitated to use his money on myself, and in the end I decided to buy gifts with it. I went to an expensive gift shop in the Ginza and chose a briar pipe for Sensei and a fancy English lighter for Tokida. I also bought a small gold pin for Michiko. While I was making the selection I noticed a carved jewelry box made of hardwood which played a little metallic tune when it was opened. I decided to send one to Reiko. I knew I meant nothing to her, and I would probably never see her again, but perhaps the gift would let her know that I still thought about her. In a way she *was* like a painting, flat and mindless. Maybe she would remember me every time she took a necklace or something out of the box. I wanted to get something for Mother as well, but didn't feel right buying her a gift with Father's money; besides, both Mother and Grandmother had asked me to leave them my oil paintings.

When I got home with the gifts I opened the music box, wound the spring and lifted the cover. A chill ran up and down my spine. *The glow of fireflies, the snow on the windowsill* . . . It was playing "Auld Lang Syne," a tune the Japanese had adopted long ago as *the* farewell song, the song children sing at graduations. I thought of running back to the store to exchange it for some other tune. Anything but this. Sending that tune to Reiko was like sending a sick person a bunch of red camellias, the symbol of decapitation. Then the irony of it dawned on me and I burst out laughing; it was a perfect gift for her. I wrapped up the box and went to the post office to mail it.

Father brought his family to Tokyo a week before our departure. My stepmother had never been outside Kyushu, and Tokyo must have seemed like a foreign country to her. She looked exactly the way I remembered her, a calm and gentle woman. I was glad to see her. My stepsister was now five years old and she didn't remember me at all.

Father took me aside and whispered to me, "I'd like to see your mother before we leave."

That surprised me. After all, he was the one who had refused to see Mother in the past.

"Will you talk to her?" asked Father.

"I'll call her and ask," I replied.

"Tomorrow will be good. Ask her if she can have lunch with us. We'll meet her in Yokohama."

He was expecting me to join them, and I didn't look forward to their meeting.

Mother was surprisingly calm when I told her.

"Tomorrow?" she said, and there was a pause. I had a feeling she was checking her calendar. "Yes, tomorrow will be fine."

"Father wants to have lunch somewhere in Yokohama."

"That's a good idea. You know where Midori's is, don't you, the restaurant near the harbor? I'll meet you there at one."

Next day Father bought first-class train tickets and we sat in silence in a nearly empty car. Noticing my silence, he became talkative, pointing out some of the landmarks that had survived the bombings. I felt like I was being an accomplice — in what I didn't know.

Mother was waiting for us outside the restaurant when we arrived. They greeted each other with a slight nod and smiled. I looked at the harbor full of foreign ships, flying colored flags. Then my parents went up the staircase, and I followed them into a bright room with large windows that looked out onto the harbor. A waiter seated us by a window.

Father was the first to speak.

"Would you like a cocktail?" he asked Mother.

"If you're having one," Mother said and took out a cigarette. Before I could strike a match Father produced a gold lighter. Though there was no wind, Mother reached with her left hand and cupped the flame and touched Father's hand. I didn't know if it was an accident, but suddenly I felt like a child, having seen the scene so many times.

"It's amazing how many places I still recognize," said Father, lighting his own cigarette.

"This neighborhood wasn't hit too badly," said Mother. "But I don't think you'd recognize the area where I have my shop."

"How is your business?"

"I'm doing very well; I may open another shop in a few months."

"A partner?"

"Yes, I have a backer."

I thought about the man I'd seen with Mother, the tall man with an angular face.

"Well, here's to your success, and to Koichi. Captain Powers sends his regards." Father lifted his glass.

"A wonderful man," said Mother, looking out the window. "He gave me my first pair of nylon stockings, do you remember? He insisted I model them for him and I wouldn't come out of the bedroom."

Father chuckled softly, remembering. We had curried rice for lunch.

"What will you do in America?" asked Mother.

"The Powerses have rented a house for us. As for business, I have some ideas, though I won't know for sure until we get there. Perhaps import-export business of some kind; I have a few associates in Tokyo who are interested. Money is not a problem, for a while at least, and should I decide to continue with my pearl business, I have all my contacts. I want to assure you that Koichi will be well taken care of; his English concerns me a little, but he's young."

"Koichi does very well in school; he was at the head of his class," said Mother.

"Is that so? He didn't tell me," he said and gave me a broad grin. Whenever I'd done something well, it was a habit of Father's to claim that I'd taken after him but he didn't say it this time.

I noticed that my parents were avoiding calling each other by name, and when their conversation bogged down they talked about me. Mother and Father, leaning over the white tablecloth, made a handsome couple. And once they had loved each other, Father giving up his job in Kobe, Mother risking disinheritance, and they had run off to Yokohama. Now they were strangers to each other, and yet I was their child, the only thing they had in common; the rest was memories. Perhaps Mr. Kubota was right; maybe love does have its own seasons: It runs its course until it is dead.

I heard Mother thank Father for taking me to America, and we walked out into the bright afternoon sun. The three of us stood on the sidewalk for a while, not knowing what more to say. I didn't know whether to go with Father or Mother.

"If you don't mind I'd like to walk around the harbor," I said finally.

"And I have to be back in Tokyo." Father looked at his watch. "You will come to see us off, won't you?" he asked Mother.

"If Yoshiko-san doesn't feel uncomfortable," she replied. Yoshiko was my stepmother.

"No, I insist that you come."

We parted, walking away in different directions. Mother turned to give me a smile, and waved. They were strangers to me as well.

❖ ❖ ❖

I hired the same man Grandmother had hired when I had first moved into my apartment, and took everything back to her house — all but the sketchbooks. I was to spend the last few days at Grandmother's house.

"So you're leaving all this with me?" said Grandmother.

"You can always give them away to your trashman," I told her.

"I will do no such thing. I'll put them away so when you decide to come back they'll be the way you left them."

"Thank you, Grandmother. I might have to ask you to send something later."

"I know you're lazy, Koichi, but write to me now and then."

"Of course I will. In English or Japanese?"

"Don't be fresh. I don't want you ever to forget your own tongue."

"Japanese then, just so I won't forget."

"Good." She gave me a smile.

❖ ❖ ❖

Michiko said nothing when I gave her the pin and a roll of my charcoal drawings.

"Won't you at least open the box and see what's inside?"

She hesitated, then unwrapped the small package.

"How lovely," she said softly and lifted the pin by the thin gold chain. "I'll always wear it, even when I sleep. But your drawings . . .

If you ever want them back, you must write to me. You will write to me, won't you?"

"Yes, and you, too."

"I'll write to you at least once a month, I promise, and tell you all the school gossip. . . . And this is for you." She handed me a small velvet-covered jewelry box. I opened it and saw a large single pearl.

"Something from Father . . . and me," she said. "It's not a cultured pearl; Father brought it back from the South Seas. I thought you could wear it with your necktie."

"Thank you. It's beautiful."

"Sei-san, when I write to you, would you mind if I address you as my brother?"

"No, I'd like that."

And with that we parted. She stood by the dog statue, holding the roll of my drawings with both hands, pressed to her body.

❖ ❖ ❖

Three days before I was to sail, Sensei took me and Tokida out to a farewell supper in a restaurant modeled after a Japanese farmhouse, with a sunken firepit on the floor and waitresses dressed like farm girls.

"Where you're going may be the wealthiest country in the world, but you're not going to find anything quite so exquisite as this in America," said Sensei.

"I thought you were going to take us to the loach place," said Tokida.

"I didn't want Kiyoi to suffer from indigestion on our last evening together," said Sensei. "Anyway, let's not talk about that now. Come, let's enjoy ourselves. Kiyoi, how long has it been since you first came to see me?"

"Going on three years, sir."

"Three years." He drew on his cigarette. "That makes me feel rather old. What did you think of us when you first came?"

"I thought you worked in a dingy place, sir. And Tokida scared me. He didn't say a word to me the whole time I was there, and I didn't think you were going to take me when you started to ask me about my parents."

"A dingy place." Sensei seemed amused. "And Tokida would've scared anybody in those days."

"You looked pretty weird yourself," said Tokida. "Barging in on us like that. That took a lot of nerve, but I knew you were scared. You were kind of jerky, looking around the room like you didn't know where you were."

"Let me say this, Kiyoi," said Sensei. "The minute I saw you I knew why you had come, and before I saw you draw I knew I was going to take you on. There was that strange look about you — a boy with his mind made up."

"Was I any good? I mean the horse you made me draw."

"I still have that drawing. One of these days I'm going to send it to you. You can look at it when you feel bad about your work, and you're going to laugh."

"Thank you for all you've done for me, Sensei."

"It is I who should thank you, and Tokida, for all the work you've done for me. I was contemplating retirement in a couple of years and letting you two take over."

He became serious.

"Kiyoi, you're going to have many masters in your life, and the most important thing to remember is to know when to leave them. Don't stay with one master too long; to do so is to limit your growth. Learn all you can from a master, and when there's nothing more to be learned, leave him; be ruthless. The only duty you have is to your art. Be true to your art. One day you too will become a master; then you must turn around and help those who seek your wisdom. One day you'll see that it's harder for the master to let go of a disciple. Remember, let your beloved child journey."

After that we walked the neon-bright streets of Tokyo as we had done so many times before. It was a beautiful city. At the train station Tokida switched his walking cane from one hand to the other and reached into his pocket.

"I almost forgot," he said. "Here."

It was the German razor his father had given him. I saw that he had spent some time polishing it.

"I can't take this," I protested.

"Take it. You're going to have to start shaving soon, take it. I'm going to buy a straightedge, and don't worry, I'm not going to cut myself."

"Thank you," I said and put the gift in my pocket.

"Well, this is sort of a temporary farewell then," said Sensei. "I won't come to see you off. I can't stand all the tape throwing and crying and all that. Stay well, Kiyoi, and write to us when you need to talk. We'll be thinking of you."

"Show them how good you are, Kiyoi. You're as good as any-body, I mean that," said Tokida, and gave me a big grin.

I stood at the ticket gate and watched their backs — Sensei in his long kimono, Tokida hobbling with his cane. Farewell, Sensei. Good-bye, Brother. I watched them until they disappeared into the crowd. I was glad they didn't look back. I was sobbing in public.

Next evening, toward sundown, I went to my apartment for the last time. The place was empty now, except for my sketchbooks. For four years the eel's bed had been mine, and I was leaving it without a trace, like a room in a cheap inn.

I took my drawings to the vacant lot next door and started a small bonfire. I tore the drawing pads and fed them to the fire and watched them burn. One by one the pages turned themselves in the miniature fire storm and nude figures, hands and legs and feet crinkled, went dark, then burst into flames. The fire made me think of my childhood. I thought about the house I was born in; it had gone up in flames. That was the end of something. And the end of the war marked something else. Then there was the divorce of my parents. Now I was leaving Mother, Sensei, and Tokida, and the country where I was born. It seemed there were many sharp breaks in my life. But the end of one phase meant the beginning of another.

In an hour's time all my drawings turned into ashes. I felt cleansed. I was ready to start a new life in a strange country.

ABOUT THE AUTHOR

Allen Say is the author and illustrator of many highly acclaimed picture books. He has won the Caldecott Medal for *Grandfather's Journey,* and a Caldecott Honor and the *Boston Globe/Horn Book* Award for *The Boy of the Three-Year Nap* (written by Dianne Snyder). His books have been chosen as Reading Rainbow selections, ALA Notable Children's Books, and *New York Times* Best Illustrated Books of the Year.